P9-CKP-553

3 1447 00740 7014

FIC
FIC
Bradley, Marion Zimmer.
Star of danger /
1993, c1965.

SF

WITHDRAWN

DATE DUE

DEC 27	OCT 04	FEB 0 2 2004
MAR 27	DEC 05	SEP 1 8 1999
JUL 20	FEB 07	OCT MAR 3 0 2004
	MAY 1 2	APR 2 3 2004
AUG 29	JAN 2	AUG 2 9 2004
	JAN 2 5 2000	NOV 1 8 2004
NOV 12		MAY JUN 0 7 2005
JAN 04	JAN 0 2	
	APR 28	OCT 0 5
JAN 3 1	SEP 2 5	NOV 1 9 AUG 3 0 2005
	OCT 2 1 2002	
FEB 18		FEB 12 2003
MAR 16		MAR 1 4 2003
APR 06		
APR 27		APR 1 2 2003
JUN 09		JUL 2 3 2003
SEP 12		AUG 2 1 2003

DEMCO 38-297

SANTA BARBARA PUBLIC LIBRARY
CENTRAL LIBRARY

STAR OF DANGER

Further Titles from Severn House
by Marion Zimmer Bradley

THE BLOODY SUN
CITY OF SORCERY
DARKOVER LANDFALL
DARK SATANIC
FALCONS OF NARABEDLA
THE INHERITOR
THE SHATTERED CHAIN
THE SPELL SWORD
WITCH HILL

STAR OF DANGER

Marion Zimmer Bradley

This first hardcover edition published in Great Britain 1993 by
SEVERN HOUSE PUBLISHERS LTD of
9–15 High Street, Sutton, Surrey SM1 1DF.
This first hardcover edition published in the U.S.A. 1993 by
SEVERN HOUSE PUBLISHERS INC., of
475 Fifth Avenue, New York, NY 10017
by arrangement with Ace Books,
an imprint of the Berkley Publishing Group Inc.

Copyright © Ace Books Inc. 1965

All rights reserved.
The moral rights of the author have been asserted.

British Library Cataloguing in Publication Data
Bradley, Marion Zimmer
    Star of Danger. – New ed
    I. Title
    813.54 [F]

    ISBN 0-7278-4513-6

Typeset by Hewer Text Composition Services, Edinburgh.
Printed and bound in Great Britain by
Redwood Books, Trowbridge, Wiltshire.

I

It didn't look much at all like an alien planet.

Larry Montray, standing on the long ramp that led downwards from the giant spaceship, felt the cold touch of sharp disillusion and disappointment. Darkover. Hundreds of light-years from Earth, a strange world under a strange sun – and it didn't look different at all.

It was night. Below him lay the spaceport, lighted almost to a daytime dazzle by rows of blue-white arclights; an enormous flat expanse of concrete ramps and runways, the blurred outlines of the giant starships dim through the lights; levels and stairways and ramps leading upward to the lines of high streets and the dark shapes of skyscrapers beyond the port. But Larry had seen spaceships and spaceports on Earth. With a father in the service of the Terran Empire, you got used to seeing things like that.

He didn't know what he'd expected of the new world – but he hadn't expected it to look just like any spaceport on Earth!

He'd expected so much . . .

Of course, Larry had always known that he'd go out into space someday. The Terran Empire had spread itself over a thousand worlds surrounding a thousand suns, and no son of Terra ever considered staying there all his life.

But he'd been resigned to waiting at least a few more years. In the old days, before star travel, a boy of sixteen could ship out as cabin boy on a windjammer, and see the world. And back in the early days of star travel, when the immense interstellar distances meant years and years in the gulfs between the stars, they'd shipped young kids to crew the starships – so they wouldn't be old men when the voyages ended.

But those days were gone. Now, a trip of a hundred

1

light-years could be made in about that many days, and men, not boys, manned the ships and the Trade Cities of the Terran Empire. At sixteen Larry had been resigned to waiting. Not happy about it. Just resigned.

And then the news had come. Wade Montray, his father, had put in for transfer to the Civil Service on the planet Darkover, far out in the edge of the Milky Way. And Larry – whose mother had died before he was old enough to remember her, and who had no other living relatives – was going with him.

He'd ransacked his school library, and all the local reading rooms, to find out something about Darkover. He didn't learn much. It was the fourth planet of a medium-sized dark red star, invisible from Earth's sky, and so dim that it had a name only in star-catalogues. It was a world smaller than Earth, it had four moons, it was a world at an arrested cultural level without very much technology or science. The major products exported from Darkover were medicinal earths and biological drugs, jewel stones, fine metals for precision tools, and a few luxury goods – silks, furs, wines.

A brief footnote in the catalogue had excited Larry almost beyond endurance: *Although the natives of Darkover are human, there are several intelligent cultures of nonhumans present on this planet.*

Nonhumans! You didn't see them often on Earth. Rarely, near one of the spaceports, you'd see a Jovian trundling by in his portable breathing-tank of methane gas; Earth's oxygen was just as poisonous to him as the gas to an Earthman. And now and again, you might catch a curious, exciting glimpse of some tall, winged man-thing from one of the outer worlds. But you never saw them up close. You couldn't think of them as *people*, somehow.

He'd badgered his father with insistent questions until his father said, in exasperation, "How should I know? I'm not an information manual! I know that Darkover has a red sun, a cold climate, and a language supposed to be derived from the old Earth languages! I know it has four moons and that there are nonhumans there – and that's all I know! So why don't you wait and find out when you get there?"

2

When Dad got that look in his eye, it was better not to ask questions. So Larry kept the rest of them to himself. But one evening, as Larry was sorting things out in his room, deciding to throw away stacks of outgrown books, toys, odds and ends he'd somehow accumulated in the last few years, his father knocked at his door.

"Busy, son?"

"Come in, Dad."

Wade Montray came in, nodding at the clutter on the bed. "Good idea. You can't take more than a few pounds of luggage with you, even these days. I've got something for you – picked it up at the Transfer Center." He handed Larry a flat package; turning it over, Larry saw that it was a set of tapes for his recording machine.

"Language tapes," his father said, "since you're so anxious to learn all about Darkover. You could get along all right in Standard, of course – everyone around the Spaceport and the Trade City speaks it. Most of the people going out to Darkover don't bother with the language, but I thought you might be interested."

"Thanks, Dad. I'll hook up the tapes tonight."

His father nodded. He was a stern-looking man, tall and quiet with dark eyes – Larry suspected that his own red hair and gray eyes came from his unremembered mother – and he hadn't smiled much lately; but now he smiled at Larry. "It's a good idea. I've found out that it helps to be able to speak to people in their own language, instead of expecting them to speak yours."

He moved the tapes aside and sat down on Larry's bed. The smile slid away and he was grave again.

"Son, do you really mind leaving Earth? It's come to me, again and again, that it's not fair to take you away from your home, out to the edge of nowhere. I almost didn't put in for that transfer thinking of that. Even now – " he hesitated. "Larry, if you'd rather, you can stay here, and I can send for you in a few years, when you're through with school and college."

Larry felt his throat go suddenly tight.

"Leave me here? On Earth?"

"There are good schools and universities, son. Nobody

3

knows what sort of education you'd be getting in quarters on Darkover.''

Larry stared straight at his father, his mouth set hard to keep it from trembling. "Dad, don't you want me along? If you – if you want to get rid of me, I won't make a fuss. But – " he stopped, swallowing hard.

"Son! Larry!" His father reached for his hands and held them, hard, for a minute. "Don't say that again, huh? Only I promised your mother you'd get a good education. And here I am dragging you halfway across the universe, off on a crazy adventure, just because I've got the itch in my bones and don't want to stay here like a sensible man. It's selfish to want to go, and worse to want to take you with me!"

Larry said, slowly, "I guess I must take after you, then, Dad. Because I don't want to stay in one spot like what you call a sensible man, either. Dad, I *want* to go. Couldn't you figure that out? I've never wanted anything so much!"

Wade Montray drew a long sigh. "I hoped you'd say that – how I hoped you'd say that!" He tossed the tapes into a pile of Larry clothes, and stood up.

"All right, son. Brush up on the language, then. There must be more than one sort of education."

Listening to the language tapes, moving his tongue around the strange fluid tones of the Darkovan speech, Larry had felt his excitement grow and grow. There were strange new concepts and thoughts in this language, and hints of things that excited him. One of the proverbs caught at his imagination with a strange, tense glow: *It is wrong to keep a dragon chained for roasting your meat.*

Were there dragons on Darkover? Or was it a proverbial phrase based on legend? What did the proverb mean? That if you had a fire-breathing dragon, it was dangerous to make him work for you? Or, did it mean that it was foolish to use something big and important for some small, silly job of work? It seemed to open up a crack into a strange world where he glimpsed unknown ideas, strange animals, new colours and thoughts through a glimmer of the unknown.

His excitement had grown with every day that passed, until they had taken the shuttle to the enormous spaceport and boarded the ship itself. The starship was huge and strange,

4

like an alien city; but the trip itself had been a let-down. It wasn't much different than a cruise by ocean liner, except that you couldn't see any ocean. You had to stay in your cabin most of the time, or in one of the cramped recreation areas. There were shots and immunizations for everything under the sun – under *any* sun, Larry corrected himself – so that he went around with a sore arm for the first two weeks of the trip.

The only moment of excitement had come early in the voyage; just after breakaway from Earth's sun, when there had been a guided tour of the ship for everyone who wasn't still struggling with acceleration sickness. Larry had been fascinated by the crew's quarters, by the high navigation deck with its rooms full of silent, brooding computers, the robots which handled, behind leaded-glass shields, any needed repairs on the drive units. He'd even seen into the drive rooms themselves, by television. They were, of course, radioactive, and even crew members could enter them only in the gravest emergencies. Most exciting of all had been the single glimpse from the Captain's bridge – the tiny glass dome with its sudden panorama of a hundred million twinkling stars. Larry, pressing himself for his brief turn against the glass, felt suddenly very lost, very small and alone in this wilderness of giant, blazing suns and worlds spinning forever against the endless dark. When he moved away he was dazed and his eyes blurred.

But the rest of the trip had been a bore. More and more he had lost himself in daydreams about the new world at the end of the journey. The very name, *Darkover*, had its curious magic. He envisioned a giant red sun lowering in a lurid sky, four moons in strange colors; his mind invented fantastic and impossible shapes for the mysterious nonhumans who would crowd around the spaceship's landing. By the time they were sent to their staterooms to strap down for the long deceleration, he was simmering with wild excitement.

He had watched the landing on TV; their approach to the planet in its veil of swirling sunset-orange clouds that had thinned into the darkness of the night side as they came near; he'd felt the shudder and surge of new gravity, the tingle of strangeness when one of the small iridescent moons swam across the camera field. He wondered which of the moons it was. Probably Kyrrdis, he thought, with its blue-green

5

shimmer, like a peacock's wing. The names of the moons were a siren song of enchantment; Kyrrdis, Idriel, Liriel, Mormallor. *We're here,* he thought, *we're really here.*

He waited, impatient but well-disciplined, for the loud-speaker announcement which permitted passengers to unfasten their straps, collect their belongings and gather in the discharge entrance. His father was silent at his side, and his face gave away nothing; Larry wondered how anyone could be so impassive, but not wanting to seem childishly eager, Larry kept silence too. He kept his eyes on the metal door which would open on the strange world. When the crewman in his black leather began undogging the seals, Larry was almost literally shaking with excitement. A strange pinkish glow filtered around the first crack of the door. *The red sun? The strange sky?*

But the door swung open on night, and the pink glow was only the fiery light of welding torches from a pit nearby, where workmen in hoods were working on the metal hull of another great ship. Larry, stepping out on to the ramp, felt the cold touch of disappointment. It was just another spaceport, just like Earth!

Behind him on the ramp, his father touched his shoulder and said, in a gently rallying tone, "Don't stand there staring, son; your new planet won't run away. I know how excited you must be, but let's move on down."

Heaving a deep sigh, Larry began to walk down the ramp. He should have known it would turn out to be a gyp. Things you build up in your mind usually were a let-down.

Later, he was to remember his sense of disillusion that morning, and laugh at himself; but at the moment, the flat disappointment was so keen he could almost taste it. The concrete felt hard and strange after weeks of uncertain gravity in the spaceship. He swayed a little to get his balance, watching the small, buzzing cargo dollies that were whirring around the field, the men in black or grayish leather uniforms with the insignia of the Terran Empire, on which the hard blue arclights reflected coldly. Beyond the lights was a dark line of tall buildings.

"The Terran Trade City," his father pointed them out. "We'll have rooms in the Quarters buildings. Come on, we'd better get checked through the lines, there's a lot of red tape."

Larry didn't feel sleepy – it had been daytime on the starship, by the arbitrary time cycle – but he was yawning by the time they got through standing in line, having their passport and credentials checked, picked up their luggage from customs. As they came away from one booth, he looked up, idly, and then his breath caught. The darkness had thinned; the sky overhead, black when he had stepped from the spaceship, was now a strange, luminous grayed-pearl. In the east, great rays of crimson light, like a vast, shimmering Aurora Borealis, began to fan out and dance through the grayness. The lights trembled as if seen through ice. Then a rim of red appeared on the horizon, gradually puffing up into an enormous, impossibly crimson sun. Blood red. Huge. Bloated. It didn't look like a sun at all; it looked like a large neon sign. The sky gradually shifted from gray to pink through the spectrum to a curious lilac-blue. In the new light the spaceport looked strange and lurid.

As the light grew, behind the line of skyscrapers Larry gradually made out a skyline of mountains – high, rough-toothed mountains with cliffs and ice-falls shining red in the sun. A pale-blue crystal of moon still hung on the shoulder of one mountain. Larry blinked, stared, kept turning to look at that impossible sun. It was still very cold; you couldn't imagine that sun warming the sky as Earth's sun did. Yet it was a huge red coal, an immense glowing fire, the color of –

"Blood. Yes, it's a bloody sun," said someone in the line behind Larry. "That's what they call it. Looks it, too."

Larry's father turned and said quietly "Seems gloomy, I know. Well, never mind, in the Trade City there will be the sort of light you're used to, and sooner or later you'll get accustomed to it." Larry started to protest, but his father did not wait for him to speak. "I've got one more line to go through. You might as well wait over there. There's no sense in you standing in line too."

Obediently, Larry got out of line and moved away. They had climbed several levels now, in their progress from line to line, and stood far above the level where the starships lay in their pits. About a hundred feet away from Larry there was a huge open archway, and he went curiously toward it, eager to see beyond the spaceport.

The archway opened on a great square, empty in the red morning light. It was floored with ancient, uneven flagstones; in the center there was a fountain, playing and splashing faintly pink. At the far end of the square, Larry saw, with a little shock of his old excitement, a line of buildings, strangely shaped, with curved stone fronts and windows of a long lozenge shape. The light played oddly on what looked like prisms of colored glass, set into the windows.

A man crossed the square. He was the first Darkovan Larry had seen; a stooped, gray-haired man wearing loose baggy breeches and a belted overshirt that seemed to be lined with fur. He cast a desultory glance at the spaceport, not seeing Larry, and slouched on by.

Two or three more men went by. Probably, Larry thought, workmen on their way to early-morning jobs. A couple of women, wearing long fur-trimmed dresses, came out of one of the buildings; one began to sweep the cobblestone sidewalk with an odd-looking fuzzy broom, while the other started to carry small tables and benches out on the walk from inside. Men lounged by; one of them sat down at a little table, signaled to one of the women, and after a time she brought him two bowls from which white steam sizzled in the frosty air. A strong pleasant smell, rather like bitter chocolate, reminded Larry that he was both cold and hungry; the Darkovan food smelled good, and he found himself wishing that he had some Darkovan money in his pocket. He remembered, experimentally, phrases in the language he had learned. He supposed he'd be able to order something to eat. The man at the table was picking up things that looked like pieces of macaroni, dipping them into the other bowl, and eating them, very tidily, with his fingers and a long pick like one chopstick.

"What are you staring at?" someone asked, and Larry started, looking up, seeing a boy a little younger than himself standing before him. "Where did you come from, *Tallo?*"

Not till the final word did Larry realize that the stranger had spoken to him in the Darkovan language, now so familiar through tapes. *Then I can understand it! Tallo* – that was the word for copper; he supposed it meant *redhead*. The strange boy was red-headed too, flaming hair cut square around a thin, handsome, dark-skinned face. He was not quite as tall as Larry. He wore a rust-colored shirt and laced-up leather jerkin, and high leather boots knee-length over close-fitting trousers. But Larry was surprised more by the fact that, at the boy's waist, in a battered leather sheath, there hung a short steel dagger.

Larry said at last, hesitantly in Darkover, "Are you speaking to me?"

"Who else?" The strange boy's hands, encased in thick dark gloves, strayed to the handle of his knife, as if absentmindedly. "What are you staring at?"

"I was just looking at the spaceport."

"And where did you get those ridiculous clothes?"

"Now look here," Larry said, taken aback at the rude tone in which the boy spoke, "why are you asking me all these questions? I'm wearing the clothes I have – and for that matter, I don't think much of yours," he added belligerently. "What is it to you, anyhow?"

The strange boy looked startled. He blinked. "But have I made a mistake? I never saw – who are you?"

"My name is Larry Montray."

The boy with the knife frowned. "I can't take it in. Do you – forgive me, but by some chance do you *belong* to the spaceport? No offense is intended but – "

"I just came in on the ship *Pantomime,*" Larry said.

The stranger frowned. He said, slowly, "That explains it, I suppose. But you speak the language so well, and you look like – you must excuse my mistake, it was natural." He stood staring at Larry for another minute. Then, suddenly, as if breaking the dam: "I've never spoken before to an off-worlder! What is it like to travel in space? Is it true that there are many suns like this one? What are the other worlds like?"

But before Larry could answer, he heard his father's voice, raised, sharply. "Larry! Where have you gotten to?"

"I'm here," he called, turning around, realizing that where he stood, he was hidden in the shadow of the archway. "Just a minute – " he turned back to the strange boy, but to his surprise and exasperation, the Darkovan boy had turned his back and was walking rapidly away. He disappeared into the dark mouth of a narrow street across the square. Larry stood frowning, looking after him.

His father came quickly toward him.

"What were you doing? Just watching the square? I suppose there's no harm, but – " He sounded agitated. "Who were you talking to? One of the natives?"

"Just a kid about my age," Larry said. "Dad, he thought – "

"Never mind now." His father cut him off, rather sharply. "We have to find our quarters and get settled. You'll learn soon enough. Come along."

Larry followed, puzzled and exasperated at his father's curtness. This wasn't like Dad. But his first disappointment at the ordinariness of Darkover had suddenly disappeared.

That kid thought I was Darkovan. Even with the clothes I was wearing. From hearing me speak the language, he couldn't tell the difference.

He looked back, almost wistfully, at the vanishing panorama of Darkover beyond the forbidden gateway. They were passing now into a street of houses and buildings that were just like Earth ones, and Larry's father sighed – with relief?

"Just like home. At least you won't be too homesick here," he said, checked the numbers on a card he held and pushed open a door. "Our rooms are in this building."

Inside, the lights had been set so that the light was that of Earth at noon, and the apartment – five rooms on the fourth floor – might have been the one they had left on Earth. All the while they were unpacking, dialing food from the dispensers, exploring the rooms, Larry's thoughts ran a new and strange pattern.

What was the point of living on a strange world if you did your best to make your house, the furniture, the very *light*, look exactly like the old one? Why not *stay* on Earth if you felt like that?

Okay, if they wanted it this way. That was okay with him. But he was going to see more of Darkover than this.

He was going to see what lay beyond that gate. The new world was beautiful, and strange – and he could hardly wait to explore it.

Homesick? What did Dad think he *was?*

II

Larry pushed back the heavy steel door of Quarters B building, and emerged into the thin cold cutting wind of the courtyard between buildings. He stood there shivering, looking at the sky; the huge red run hung low, slowly dropping toward the horizon, where thin ice-clouds massed in mountains of crimson and scarlet and purple.

Behind him Rick Stewart shivered audibly, pulling his coat tight. "Brrr, I wish they had a passageway between the buildings! And I can't see a thing in this light. Let's get inside, Larry." He waited a minute, impatiently. "What are you staring at?"

"Nothing." Larry shrugged and followed the other lad into Quarters A, where their rooms were located. How could he say that this brief daily passage between Quarters B – where the school for spaceport youngsters, from kindergarten to pre-university, was located – and Quarters A, was his only chance to look at Darkover?

Inside in the cool yellow Earthlike light, Rick relaxed. "You're an odd one," he said, as they took the elevator to their floor. "I'd think the light out there would hurt your eyes."

"No, I like it. I wish we could get out and explore."

"Well, shall we go down to the spaceport?" Rick chuckled. "There's nothing to see there but starships, and they're an old story to me, but I suppose to you they're still exciting."

Larry felt exasperated at the patronizing amusement in Rick's voice. Rick had been on Darkover three years – and frankly admitted that he had never been beyond the spaceport. "Not that," he said, "I'd like to get into the town – see what it's like." His pent-up annoyance suddenly escaped. "I've been on Darkover three weeks, and I might as well be back on Earth!

Even here in the school, I'm studying the same things I was studying at home! History of Terra, early Space Exploration, Standard Literature, mathematics – "

"You bet," Rick said. "You don't think any Terran citizens would stay here, if their kids couldn't get a decent education, do you? Requirements for any Empire university."

"I know that. But after all, living on this planet, we should know a little something about it, shouldn't we?"

Rick shrugged again. "I can't imagine why." They came into the rooms Larry shared with his father, and dumped their school books and paraphernalia. Larry went to the food dispenser – from which food prepared in central kitchens was delivered by pneumatic tube and charged to their account – and dialed himself a drink and a snack, asking Rick what he wanted. The boys stretched out on the furniture, eating hungrily.

"You *are* an odd one," Rick repeated. "Why do you care about this planet? We're not going to stay here all our lives. What good would it do to learn everything about it? What we get in the Terran Empire schools will be valid on any Empire planet where they send us. As for me, I'm going into the Space Academy when I'm eighteen – and goodness knows, that's reason enough to hit the books on navigation and math!"

Larry munched a cracker. "It just seems funny," he repeated with stubborn emphasis, "to live on a world like this and not know more about it. Why not *stay* on Earth, if their culture is the only one you care about?"

Rick's chuckle was tolerant. "This is your first planet out from Earth? Oh, well, that explains it. After you've seen a couple, you'll realize that there's nothing out there but a lot of barbarians and outworlders. Unless you're going in for archaeology or history as a career, why clutter up your mind with the details?"

Larry couldn't answer. He didn't try. He finished his cracker and opened his book on navigation. "Was this the problem that was bothering you?"

But while they put their heads together, figuring out interstellar orbits and plotting collision curves, Larry was still thinking with frustrated eagerness of the world outside – the world, it seemed now, he'd never know.

Rick didn't seem to care. None of the youngsters he'd met here in the Trade City seemed to care. They were Earthmen, and anything outside the Terran Zone was alien – and they couldn't have cared less. They lived the same life they'd have lived on any Empire planet, and that was the way they wanted it.

They'd even been surprised – no, thunderstruck – to hear that he'd learned the Darkovan speech. They couldn't imagine why. One of the teachers had been faintly sympathetic; he'd shown Larry how to make the complicated letters of the Darkovan alphabet, and even loaned him a few books written in Darkovan. But there wasn't much time for that. Mostly he got the same schooling he'd have had on Earth. Darkover, even the light of Darkover's red sun, was barriered out by walls and yellow earth-type lights; and the closed minds of the Terran Zone personnel were even more of a barrier.

When Rick had gone, Larry put his books away and sat scowling, thinking it over, until his father came in.

"How's it going, Dad?"

He was fascinated by his father's work, but Wade Montray wouldn't talk about it much. Larry knew that his father worked in the customs office, and that his work was, in a general way, to see that no contraband was smuggled from Darkover to the Terran Zone, or vice versa. It sounded interesting to Larry, though his father kept insisting it was not much different from the work he'd done on Earth.

But today he seemed somewhat more communicative.

"How about dialing us some supper? I was too busy, today, to stop and eat. We had some trouble at the Bureau. One of the City Elders came to us, as mad as a drenched cat. He insisted that one of our men had carried weapons into the City, and we had to check it up. What happened was that some young fool of a Darkovan had offered one of the Spaceport Guards a lot of money to sell him one of his pistols and report it lost. When we checked with the man, sure enough, he'd done just that. Of course, he lost his rank and he'll be on the next spaceship out of Darkover. The confounded fool!"

"Why, Dad?"

Wade Montray leaned his chin on his hands. "You don't know much Darkovan history, do you? They have a thing

13

called the Compact, signed a thousand years ago, which makes it illegal for anyone to have or to use any weapons except the kind which brings the man who uses it into the same risk as the man he attacks with it."

"I don't think I quite understand that, Dad."

"Well, look. If you wear a sword, or a knife, in order to use it, you have to get close to your victim – and for all you know, *he* may have a knife and be better than you are at using it. But guns, shockers, blasters, atomic bombs – you can use those without taking any risk of getting hurt yourself. Anyway, Darkover signed the Compact, and before they agreed to let the Terran Empire build a spaceport here for trade, we had to give them iron-clad guarantees that we'd help them keep contraband out of Darkover."

"I don't blame them," Larry said. He had heard the tales of the early planetary wars on Earth.

"Anyway. The man who bought this gun from our space-force guard has a collection of rare old weapons, and he swears he only wanted it as part of his collection – but nobody can be sure of that. Contraband *does* get across the border some-times, no matter how careful we are. So I had quite a day trying to trace it down. Then I had to arrange for a couple of students from the medical schools here to go out into the back country on Darkover, studying diseases. We've arranged to admit a few Darkovans to the medical schools here. Their medical science isn't up to much, and they think very highly of our doc-tors. But it isn't easy even then. The more superstitious natives are prejudiced against anything Terran. And the higher caste Darkovans won't have anything to do with us because it's beneath their dignity to associate with aliens. They think we're barbarians. I talked to one of their aristocrats today and he behaved as if I smelled bad." Wade Montray sighed.

"They think we're barbarians," Larry said slowly, "and here in the Terran Zone, we think *they* are."

"That's right. And there doesn't seem to be any answer."

Larry put down his fork. He burst out, suddenly, "Dad, when am I going to get a chance to see something of Darkover?" All his frustration exploded in him. "All this time, and I saw more through a gate on the spaceport than I've seen since!"

His father leaned back and looked at him curiously. "Do you want to see it so much?"

Larry made it an understatement. "I do."

His father sighed. "It's not easy," he said. "The Darkovans don't especially like having Terrans here. We're more or less expected to keep to our own Trade Cities."

"But why?"

"It's hard to explain," said Wade Montray, shaking his head. "Mostly they're afraid of our influence on them. Of course they're not all like that, but enough of them are."

Larry's face fell, and his father added, slowly, "I can try to get permission, sometime, to take you on a trip to one of the other Trade Cities; you'd see the country in between. As for the Old Town near the spaceport – well, it's rather a rough section, because all the spacemen in from the ships spend their furloughs there. They're used to Earthmen, of course, but there isn't much to see." He sighed again. "I know how you feel, Larry. I suppose I can take you to see the market, if that will get rid of this itch you have to see something outside the Terran Zone."

"When? Now?"

His father laughed. "Get a warm coat, then. It gets cold here, nights."

The sun hung, a huge low red ball on the rim of the world, as they crossed the Terran Zone, threaded the maze of the official buildings and came out at the edge of the levels which led downward to the spaceports. They did not go down toward the ships, but instead walked along the highest level. They passed the gate where – once before – Larry had stood to look out at the city; only this time they went on past that gate and toward another one, at the far edge of the port.

This gate was larger, and guarded by black-clad men armed with holstered weapons. Both of the guards nodded in recognition at Larry's father as they went through into the open square.

"Don't forget the curfew, Mr. Montray. All Zone personnel not on duty are supposed to be inside the gates by midnight, our time."

Montray nodded. As they crossed the square side by side,

15

he asked. "How are you getting along on the new sleep cycle, Larry?"

"It doesn't bother me." Darkover had a twenty-eight hour period of rotation, and Larry knew that some people found it difficult to adjust to longer days and nights, but he hadn't had any trouble.

The open square between the spaceport and the Darkovan city of Thendara was wide, open to the sky, and darkly spacious in the last red light of the sun. At one side it was lighted with the arclights from the spaceport; at the other side, it was already dimly lit with paler lights in a medium pinkish color. At the far end there was a row of shops, and Darkovans and Earthmen were moving about in front of them. The wares displayed were of a bewildering variety: furs, pottery dishes, ornate polished knives with bright sheaths, all kinds of fruits, and what looked like sweets and candies. But as Larry paused to inspect them, his father said in a low voice. "This is just the tourist section – the overflow from the spaceport. I thought you'd rather see the old market. You can come here any time."

They turned into a sidestreet floored with uneven cobblestones, too narrow for any sort of vehicle. His father walked swiftly, as if he knew where he was going, and Larry thought, not without resentment, *He's been here before. He knows just where to go. Yet he never realized that I'd want to see all this, too.*

The houses on either side were low, constructed of stone for the most part, and seemed very old. They all had a great many windows with thick, translucent, colored or frosted glass set in patterns into the panes, so that nothing could be seen from outside. Between the houses were low stalls made of reeds or wood, and a variety of outbuildings. Larry wondered what the houses were like inside. As he passed one of them, there was a strong smell of roasting meat, and behind one of the houses he heard the voices of children playing. A man rode slowly down the street, mounted on a small brownish horse; Larry realized that he controlled the horse without bit or bridle, with only a halter and the reins.

The narrow street widened and came out into a much larger open space, filled with the low reed stalls, canvas tents with many-coloured awnings, or small stone kiosks. It was dimly

16

lighted with the flaring enclosed lights. Around the perimeter of the market, horses and carts were tied, and Larry looked at them curiously.

"Horses?"

Montray nodded. "They don't manufacture any surface transport of any sort. We've tried to get them interested in a market for autocars or helicopters, but they say they don't like building roads and nobody is in a hurry anyway. It's a barbarian world, Larry. I told you that. Between ourselves," he lowered his voice, "I think many of the Darkovan people would like some of our kind of machinery and manufacturing. But the people who run things want to keep their world just the way it is. They like it better that way."

Larry was looking around in fascination. He said, "I'd hate to see this market turned into a big mechanized shopping center, though. The ones on Earth are ugly."

His father smiled. "You wouldn't like it if you had to live with it," he said. "You're like all youngsters, you romanticize old-fashioned things. Believe me, the Darkovan authorities aren't romantic. It's just easier for them to go on running things their own way, if they keep the people doing things the way they always have. But it won't last long." He sounded quietly certain. "Once the Terran Empire comes in to show people what a star-travel civilization can be like, people will want progress."

A tall hard-faced man in a long, wrapped cloak gave them a sharp, angry glance from harsh blue eyes, then lowered thick eyelashes and walked past them. Larry looked up at his father.

"Dad, that man heard what you said, and he didn't like it!"

"Nonsense," his father said. "I wasn't speaking that loud, and very few of them can speak Terran languages. It's all part of the same thing. They trade with us, yet they want nothing to do with our culture." He stopped beside a row of stalls. "Can you see anything you'd like here?"

There was a row of blue-and-white glazed bowls in small and larger sizes, a similar row of green-and-brown ones. At the next stall there were knives and daggers of various sorts, and Larry found himself thinking of the Darkovan boy who had worn a knife in his belt. He picked up one and fingered it idly; at his father's frown, he laughed a little and put it back. What would he do with it? Earthmen didn't wear swords!

An old woman behind a low counter was bending over a huge pottery bowl of steaming, bubbling fat, twisting strips of dough and dropping them into the oil. Below the bowl, the charcoal fire glowed like the red sun, throwing out a welcome heat to where the boy stood. The strips of dough twisted like small goldfish as they turned crisp and brown; as she fished them out, Larry felt suddenly hungry. He had not spoken Darkovan since that first day, but as he opened his mouth, he found that the learning-tapes had done their work well, for he knew just what he wanted to say, and how.

"What is the price of your cakes, please?"

"Two sekals for each, young sir," she said, and Larry, fishing in his pocket for his spending money, asked for half a dozen. His father put down a scroll at the next stall, and came toward him.

"Those are very good," he said. "I've tasted them. Something like doughnuts."

The old woman was laying out the cakes on a clean coarse cloth, letting the sweet-smelling oil drain from them, dusting them with some pale stuff. She wrapped them in a sheet of brownish fiber and handed the package to Larry.

"Your accent is strange, young sir. Are you from the Cahuenga ranges?" As she raised her lined old face, Larry saw with a shock that the woman's eyes were whitish and unfocused; she was blind. *But she had thought his speech genuinely Darkovan!* He made a noncommital reply, paying her for the cakes and biting hungrily into one. They were hot, sweet and crisp, powdered lightly with what tasted like crushed rock candy.

They moved down the twilit lane of booths. Now and again they encountered uniformed men from the spaceport, or occasional civilians, but most of the men, women and children in the market were Darkovans, and they regarded the Terrans, father and son, with faintly hostile curiosity.

Larry thought, *Everyone stares at us. I wish I could dress like a Darkovan and mix in with them somehow so they wouldn't take any notice of me. Then I could know what they were really*

18

like. Gloomily he munched the doughnut cake, stopping to look over at a display of short knives.

The Darkovan behind the stall said to Larry's father, "Your son is not yet of an age to bear weapons. Or do you Terrans not allow your young men to be men?" His smile was sly, faintly patronizing, and Larry's father frowned and looked irritated.

"Are you about ready to go, Larry?"

"Any time you say, Dad." Larry felt faintly deflated and let down. What, after all, had he been expecting? They turned back, making their way along the row of stalls.

"What did that fellow mean, Dad?"

"On Darkover you'd be legally of age – old enough to wear a sword. And expected to use them to defend yourself, if necessary," Wade Montray said briefly.

Abruptly and with a rush, the red sun sank and went out. Immediately, like sweeping wings, darkness closed over the sky, and thin swirling coils of mist began to blow along the alleys of the market. Larry shivered in his warm coat, and his father pulled up his collar. The lights of the market danced and flickered, surrounded by foggy shapes of color.

"That's why they call the planet Darkover," Larry's father said. Already he was half invisible in the mist. "Stay close to me or you'll get lost in the fog. It will thin out and turn to rain in a few minutes, though."

Through the thick mist, in the flickering lights, a form took shape, coming slowly toward them. At first it looked like a tall man, cloaked and hooded against the cold; then, with a strange prickling along his spine, Larry realized that the hunched, high-shouldered form beneath the cloak was not human. A pair of green eyes, luminescent as the eyes of a cat by lamplight, knifed in their direction. The non-human came slowly on. Larry stood motionless, half-hypnotized, held back by those piercing eyes, almost unable to move.

"Get back!" Roughly, his father jerked him against the wall; Larry stumbled, sprawled, fell, one hand flung out to get his balance. The hand brushed the edge of the alien's cloak –

A stinging, violent pain rocked him back, thrust him, with a harsh blow, against the stone wall. It was like the shock of a naked electric wire. Speechless with pain, Larry picked himself up. The nonhuman, unhurried, was gliding

19

slowly away. Wade Montray's face was dead white in the flickering light.

"Larry! Son, are you hurt?"

Larry rubbed his hand; it was numb and it prickled. "I guess not. What was that thing, anyhow?"

"A *Kyrri*. They have protective electric fields, like some kinds of fish on earth." His father looked somber. "I haven't seen one in a human town for years."

Larry, still numbed, gazed after the dwindling form with respect and strange awe. "One thing's for sure, I won't get in their way again," he said fervently.

The mist was thinning and a fine spray of icy rain was beginning to fall. Not speaking, Wade Montray hurried toward the spaceport; walking fast to keep up – and not minding, because it was freezing cold and the rapid pace kept him warm – Larry wondered why his father was so silent. Had he simply been afraid? It seemed more than that.

Montray did not speak again until they were within their own rooms in Quarters A, the warmth and bright yellow light closing around them like a familiar garment. Larry, laying his coat aside, heard his father sigh.

"Well, does that satisfy your curiosity a little, Larry?"

"Thanks, Dad."

Montray dropped into a chair. "That means no. Well, I suppose you can visit the tourist section and the market by yourself, if you want to. Though you'd better not do too much wandering around alone."

His father dialed himself a hot drink from the dispenser, came back sipping it. Then he said, slowly, "I don't want to tie strings on you, Larry. I'll be honest with you; I wish you hadn't been cursed with that infernal curiosity of yours. I'd like it better if you were like the other kids here – content to stay an Earthman. It would take a load of my mind. But I'm not going to forbid you to explore if you want to. You're old enough, certainly, to know what you want. If you'd been brought up here, you'd be considered a grown man – old enough to wear a sword and fight your own duels."

"How did you know that, Dad?"

His father did not look at him. Facing the wall, he said, "I

20

spent a few years here before you were born. I never should have come back. I knew that. Now I can see – "

He broke off sharply, and without another word, he went off into his own bedroom. Larry did not see him again that night.

III

If Larry's father had hoped that this glimpse of Darkover would dim Larry's hunger for the world outside the Terran Zone, he was mistaken. The faint, far-off glance at strangeness had whetted Larry's curiosity without satisfying it.

But after all, he didn't forbid me to leave the Terran Zone. Larry told himself that, defiantly, every time he crossed the gates of the spaceport and went out into the city. He knew his father disapproved, but they never spoke of it.

On foot, alone, he explored the strange city; at first staying close to the walls of the spaceport, within sight of the tall landmark-beacon of the Quarters Buildings. Terrans were a familiar sight, and the Darkovans of the sector paid little attention to the tall, red-haired young Terran. Some of the shopkeepers, when they found that he could speak their language, were inclined to be friendly.

Heartened by these expeditions into the city, Larry gradually grew bolder. Now and again he ventured out of the familiar spaceport district, exploring an unusually alluring side street, walking through an unfamiliar court or square.

One afternoon he stood for an hour near the door of a forge, watching a blacksmith shoeing one of the small, sturdy Darkovan horses with light strong metal shoes. You didn't see things like that on Earth, not in this day and age. Horses were rare animals, kept in zoos and museums.

He was aware, now and then, of curious or hostile glances following him. Terrans were not overly popular in the city. But he had been brought up on Earth, a quiet and well-policed world, and hardly knew what fear was. Certainly, he thought, he was safe on the public streets during the daylight hours!

*   *   *

22

It was a few days after he had watched the blacksmith at work. He had gone back to that quarter, fascinated by the sight; and then, lured by a street lined with gardens of strange, low-hanging trees and flowers, he had walked down court after court. After a time, he began to realize that he had taken little heed of his bearings; the street had turned and twisted several times, and he was no longer very sure which way he had come. He looked around, but the high houses nearby concealed the beacons of the spaceport, and he was not sure which way to go.

Larry did not panic. He felt sure that he need only retrace his steps a little way to come back into familiar ground; or, perhaps, to go on a little further, and he would come out into a part of the city that he knew.

He went on a little way. The garden street suddenly ran out, and he found himself in a part of the city where he had never been before. It was so unlike anything he had seen so far that he seriously began to wonder if he had strayed into a nonhuman district. The sun was low in the sky and Larry began to worry a little about it. Could he, after all, find his way?

He looked around, trying to orient himself in the dimming light. The streets were irregular here, and twisting; the houses close together, made of thatch and chinked pebbles daubed with what looked like coarse cement, windowless and dark. The street seemed empty; and yet, as he stopped and looked around, Larry had the disconcerting notion that someone was watching him.

"Come on," he said aloud, "don't start imagining things."

He started seriously to take stock of his position. The spaceport lay to the east of the town, so that he should put his back to the sun, and keep on going that way.

Somebody's watching me. I can feel it.

He turned around slowly, getting his bearings. He ought to turn this way, into this street, and keep on eastward, then he couldn't possibly miss the spaceport. It might be a long walk, but before long he ought to get into some familiar district. *Before dark, I hope.* He looked back, nervously, as he turned into the narrow street. Was that a step behind him?

He ordered himself to stop imagining things. *People live here. They have a right to walk down the street, so what*

23

if there is somebody behind you? Anyway, there's nobody there.

Abruptly the street turned a blind corner, ran into a small open square, and dead-ended in a low stone wall and the blank rear entrances of a couple of houses. Larry scowled, and felt like swearing. He'd have to try again, damn it! And if the sun went down and he had to start wandering round in the dark, he'd be in fine shape! He turned to retrace his steps, and stopped dead.

Across the square, several indistinct forms were coming toward him. In the lowering light, purple-edged, they seemed big and looming, and they seemed to advance on Larry with steady purpose. He started to walk on, then hesitated; they were moving – yes, they had cut off his return from the way he had come.

He could see them clearly now. They were boys and young men, six or eight of them, about his own age or a little younger, shabbily dressed in Darkovan clothes; their rough-cut hair was lying on their shoulders, and one and all, they had a look of jeering malice. They looked rough, rowdy, and not at all friendly, and Larry felt a touch of panic. But he told himself, sternly, *They're just a batch of kids. Most of them look younger than I am. Why should I assume they're after me – or that they have any interest in me at all? For all I know, they might be the local chowder and marching society, out for an evening on the town!*

He nodded politely, and began to walk toward them, confident that they would part and let him through. Instead, the ranks suddenly closed, and Larry had to stop to keep from bumping headlong into the leader – a big, burly boy of sixteen or so.

Larry said politely, in Darkovan, "Will you let me pass, please?"

"Why, he talks our lingo!" The burly boy's dialect was so rough that Larry could hardly make out the words. "And what's a *Terranan* from behind the walls doing out here in the city?"

"What you want here anyway?" one of the young men asked.

Larry braced himself hard, trying not to show fear, and

24

spoke with careful courtesy. "I was walking in the city, and lost myself. If one of you would tell me which way I should take to find the spaceport, I would be grateful."

The polite speech, however, was greeted with guffaws of shrill laughter.

"Hey, he's lost!"

"Ain't that too bad!"

"Hey, *chiyu*, you expect the big boss of the spaceport to come looking for you with a lamp?"

"Poor little fellow, out alone after dark!"

"And not even big enough to carry a knife! Does your mammy know you're out walking, little boy?"

Larry made no answer. He was beginning to be dreadfully afraid. They might simply take it out in rough language – but they might not. These Darkovan street urchins might be just children – but they carried wicked long knives, and they were evidently toughs. He began to measure the leader with his eyes, wondering if he could stand up to them if it came to a fight. He might – the big bully looked fat and out of condition – but he certainly couldn't handle the whole gang of them at once.

Just the same, he knew that if he showed fear once, he was lost. If they were simply baiting him, a bold manner might bluff them away. He clenched his fists, trying with the gesture to hold his voice tight, and stepped up to the bully.

"Get out of my way."

"Suppose you *knock* me out of it, Terran!"

"Okay," said Larry between his teeth, "you asked for it, fat guy."

Quickly, with one hard punch, he drove his fist into the big boy's chin. The youngster let out a surprised "Ugh!" of pain, but his own fists came up, driving a low, foul blow into Larry's stomach. Larry, shocked as well as hurt, was taken aback. He staggered to recover his balance, gasping for breath.

The big boy kicked him. Then, in a rush, the whole gang was on him, shoving and jostling him rudely, yelling words Larry did not understand. They shouldered him back, hustling him, forming a circle around him, pushing him off balance every time he recovered it, closing in to shove and jeer. Larry's breath came in sobs of rage.

25

"*One* of you fight me, you cowards, and you'll see – "

A kick landed in his shins; someone drove an elbow into his stomach. He slid to his knees. A fist jammed into his face, and he felt blood break from his lip. Cold terror suddenly gripped through him as he realized that no one in the Terran Zone so much as knew where he was; that he could be not only mauled but killed.

"Get away from him, you filthy gutter rabbits!"

It was a new voice, clear and contemptuous, striking through the rude jeers and yells. With little gulps and gasps of consternation, the street urchins jostled back, and Larry, coming up slowly to his knees, wiping at his bloody face in the respite, blinked in the sudden light of torches.

Two tall men, green-clad, stood there carrying lights; but the lights, and all eyes, were focused on the young man who stood between the torches.

He was tall and red-haired, dressed in an embroidered leather jacket and a short fur coat; his hand was on the hilt of a knife. His eyes, cold gray, were blazing as he whipped them with stinging words:

"Nine – ten against one, and he was still giving a good account of himself to you! So this proves that Terrans are cowards, eh?"

His eyes swung to Larry, and he gestured. "Get up."

The fat bully-boy was literally shaking. He bowed his head, whining, "Lord Alton – "

The newcomer silenced him with a gesture. The smaller roughnecks looked sullen or overawed. The youngster in the fur cloak took a step toward Larry, and a cold, bleak smile touched his lips.

"I might have known it would be you," he said. "Well, we're under bond to keep peace in the city, but it seems to me you were asking for trouble. What were you doing here?"

"Walking," Larry said. "I got lost." Suddenly he resented the cool, arrogant air of authority in the newcomer's voice. He flung his head back, set his chin and looked the strange boy straight in the eye. "Is that a crime?"

The fur-cloaked boy laughed briefly, and suddenly Larry recognized the laugh and the face. It was the same insolent redhead he had seen his first day on Darkover; the youngster who'd spoken to him at the spaceport gate.

The Darkovan boy looked around at the little knot of roughs, who had drawn back and were shouldering one another restlessly. "Not so brave now, eh? Don't worry, I didn't come to stop your fight," he said, and his voice was contemptuous and clear. "But you might as well make it mean something." He looked back at Larry, then back to the gang. "Pick out someone of your number – someone his own size – and *one* of you will take him on." His eyes raked Larry's and he added, consideringly. "Unless you're afraid to fight, Terran? Then I can send you home with my bodyguards."

Larry bristled at the suggestion. "I'll fight any five of them, if they fight fair," he said angrily, and the Darkovan threw back his head with a sharp laugh.

"One's plenty. All right, you bully boys," he snarled suddenly at the gang, "pick out your champion. Or isn't any one of you willing to stand up to a Terran without the whole rat-pack behind you?"

The street boys crowded together, looking warily at Larry, and the two looming guards, at the young Darkovan aristocrat. There was a long moment of silence. The Darkovan laughed, very softly.

Finally one of the gang, a long lean young man almost six feet tall, with a broken tooth and a rangy, yellowed, evil face, spat on the cobblestones.

"I'll fight the – " Larry did not understand the epithet. "I'm not afraid of any Terran from 'ere to the Hellers!"

Larry clenched his fists, sizing up his new opponent. He supposed the street boy was a year or so older than himself. Tall and stringy, with huge fists, he looked a nasty customer. This wasn't going to be easy either.

Suddenly the boy rushed him, landing a pounding succession of blows before Larry could counter a single punch. Larry was forced backward. One fist smashed into his eye; a second landed on his chin. He struggled to stay upright, hearing the street toughs yelling encouragement to their mate. The sound suddenly made Larry angry. He rushed forward, head down, and brought up his fist in a hard, rocking blow to the roughneck's chin; followed it up with a fast punch to the nose.

27

The street boy's nose began to trickle blood. He struck out at Larry, furiously, but Larry, his rage finally roused, easily countered the wildly flailing blows. He realized that in spite of the street boy's longer reach, he didn't have the advantage of knowing what he was doing. The ruffian got in one or two low body punches, but Larry, carefully mustering his knowledge of boxing, slowly forced him back and back, stepping on his toes, keeping him off balance, driving punch after punch at the boy's nose and chin. Head down, the roughneck tried to clinch; grabbed Larry around the waist and grappled with him, struggling to bring his knee up; but Larry knocked his elbow across the boy's face, managed to pry him loose, and drove up one single, hard punch in the eye.

The street boy reeled back, swayed, stumbled and crashed down full length on the cobblestones.

"Come on," said Larry, standing over him in a rage. "Get up and fight!"

The tough stirred. He struggled halfway to his knees, swayed again and collapsed in a heap.

Larry draw a long breath. His mouth was split and tasted of blood, his eye hurt, and his ribs were bruised; and his fists, knuckles skinned raw, felt as if he'd been banging on a brick wall with them.

The Darkovan aristocrat motioned to one of his body-guards, who bent to look at the unconscious street boy.

"Now, the rest of you tough fellows – make yourselves scarce!" His voice held stinging contempt. One by one, the gang melted away into the lowering mists of darkness.

Larry stood with his knuckles throbbing, until no one was left in the square but himself, the Darkovan boy, and the two silent guards.

"Thanks,"he said, at last.

"No need to thank me," the Darkovan lad said brusquely. "You handled yourself well. I wanted to see how you'd come off." Suddenly, he smiled. "As far as I'm concerned, you've earned the freedom of the city. You've done something to deserve it. I've had an eye on you for several days, you know."

Larry stared. "What?"

"Do you think a redheaded Terran can walk in places where

no other Terran ever dared to go, without half the city knowing it? And things come to the ears of the *Comyn*."

Comyn . . . Larry didn't know the word.

The boy went on, "I was sure it was only a matter of time until you got into trouble, and I wanted to see whether you'd handle it like the typical Terran" – again there was a trace of contempt in his voice – "and try to scare off your attackers with cowards' weapons, like your guards with their guns, or shout for the police to come and help you out of your troubles. No Terran ever settles his own affairs." Then he grinned. "But you did."

"I couldn't have without your help, though."

The boy shook his head in disclaimer. "I didn't lift a hand. I only made sure that the settlement was an honourable one – and as far as I'm concerned, you can go where you like in the city from now on. My name is Kennard Alton. What's yours?"

"Larry Montray."

Kennard spoke a formal Darkovan phrase, inclining his head. Then, suddenly, he grinned.

"My father's house is only a few steps away," he said, "and I'm off duty for the night. You can't possibly go back to the Terran Zone looking like that!" For the first time, he looked as young as he was, the formal soberness disappearing in boyish laughter. "You'd frighten your people out of their wits – and if your mother and father worry the way mine do, it's nothing to look forward to! Anyway, you'd better come home with me."

Without waiting for Larry's answer, he turned, motioning to his guards, and Larry, following without a word, felt a smothered excitement. What had looked like a nasty situation was turning into an adventure. Actually invited into a Darkovan house!

Kennard led the way to one of the high houses. A wide, low-walled garden surrounded it; there were flights of stone steps up which Kennard led Larry. He made some curious gesture and the door swung wide; he turned.

"Enter and welcome; come in peace, Terran."

The moment seemed to demand a formal acknowledgment, but Larry could only say, "Thank you." He stepped into the wide hall of a brightly-lit house, blinking in the brilliant entry-way, and looking around with curiosity and wonder.

Someone, somewhere, was playing on a stringed instrument that sounded like a harp. The floors under his feet were translucent stone; the walls were hung with bright thin panels of curtain. A tall, furry nonhuman with green intelligent eyes came forward and took Kennard's cloak, and at a signal, took Larry's torn jacket also.

"It's my mother's reception night, so we won't bother her," Kennard said, and, turning to the nonhuman, added, "Tell my father I have a guest upstairs."

Larry followed Kennard up another long flight. Kennard flung open a dark door, hummed a low note, and the room was filled suddenly with bright light and warmth.

It was a pleasant room. There were low couches and chairs, a rack of knives and swords against the wall, a stuffed bird that looked like an eagle, a framed painting of a horse, and, on a small high table, something that looked like a chessboard or checkerboard with crystal pieces set up at each end. The room was luxurious, but for all that it was not tidy; various odds and ends of clothing were strewn here and there, and there was a table piled high with odd items Larry could not identify. Kennard threw open another door, and said, "Here. Your face is all blood, and your clothes are a mess. You'd better clean up a little, and you might as well put on some of my things for the time being." He rummaged behind a panel, flung some curiously shaped garments at Larry. "Come back when you're presentable."

The room was a luxurious bathroom, done in tile of a dozen colors, set in geometric patterns. The fixtures were strange, but after a little experimenting, Larry found a hotwater faucet, and washed his face and hands. The warm water felt good on his bruised face, and he realized – looking into a long mirror – that between the gang-jostling and the fight, he had really been given quite a roughing up! He began to worry a little. What would his father say?

Well, he'd *wanted* to see Darkovan life close at hand, and he'd worry about getting home late, some other time! Dad would understand when he explained. He took off his torn and dirty clothes, and got into the soft wool trousers and the

30

fur-lined jerkin which Kennard had lent him. He looked at himself in the mirror; why, except for his red hair, cut short, he might be any young Darkovan! Come to think of it, except for Kennard, he hadn't seen any red-haired Darkovans. But there must be some!

When he came out, Kennard was lounging in one of the chairs, a small table drawn up before him with several steaming bowls of food on it. He motioned to Larry to sit down.

"I'm always starved when I come off duty. Here, have something to eat." He hesitated, looking a little curiously at Larry as the other picked up the bowl and the long pick like a chopstick, then laughed. "Good, you can manage these. I wasn't sure."

The food was good, small meat rolls stuffed with something like rice or barley; Larry ate hungrily, dipping his rolls in the sharp fruity pickle-sauce as Kennard did. At last he put down the bowl and said, "You told me you've been watching me, while I've been exploring the city. Why?"

Kennard reached for the bowl containing some small crisp sticky things, took a handful and passed them to Larry before answering. He said, "I don't quite know how to say it without insulting you."

"Go ahead," Larry said. "Look, you probably saved me from getting pretty badly hurt, if not killed. Say anything you want to. I'll try not to take offense."

"This is nothing against you. But nobody in Thendara wants trouble. Terrans have been mauled or murdered, here in the city. They usually bring it on themselves. I don't mean that you would have brought anything on yourself – those street boys are alley rats and they'll attack perfectly harmless people. But other Terrans *have* made trouble in the city, and our people have treated them as they deserve. So it should be settled – a troublemaker has been punished, and the affair is over. But you Terrans simply will not accept that. Any time one of your people is hurt, no matter what he had done to deserve it, your spaceforce men come around prying into the whole matter, raking up a scandal, insisting on long trials and questioning and punishment. On Darkover, any man who's man enough to wear breeches instead of skirts is supposed to be able to protect himself; and if he can't, it's an affair for his family

31

to settle. Our people find it hard to understand your ways. But we have made a treaty with the Terrans, and responsible people here in the city don't want trouble. So we try to prevent incidents of that sort – when we can do it honorably."

Larry munched absentmindedly on one of the sweet things. They were filled with tart fruit, like little pies. He was beginning to see the contrast between his own world – orderly, with impersonal laws – and Darkover, with a fierce and individualistic code of every man for himself. When the two clashed –

"But it was more than that," Kennard said. "I was curious about you. I've been curious about you since the first day I saw you at the spaceport. Most of you Terrans like to stay behind your walls – they won't even take the trouble to learn our language! Why are you different?"

"I don't know. I don't know why they are the way they are, either. Just – well, call it curiosity." Something else occurred to Larry. "So you didn't just *happen* to come along then? You've been watching me?"

"Off and on. But it was just luck I came along then. I was off duty and coming home, and heard the racket in the square. And, on duty or off, that's part of my work."

"Your work?"

Kennard said, "I'm a cadet officer in the City Guard. All the boys in my family start as cadets, when they're fourteen winters old, working three days in the cycle as peace officers. Mostly, I just supervise guards and check over the duty lists. What sort of work do you do?"

"I don't do any work yet. I just go to school." It made him feel, suddenly, very young and ill at ease. This self-possessed youngster, no older than Larry himself, was already doing a man's work – not frittering his time away, being treated like a schoolboy!

"And then you have to start in doing your man's work full time, without any training? How strange," Kennard said.

"Well, your system seems strange to me," Larry said, with a flare of resentment against Kennard's assumption that *his* way was the proper one, and Kennard grinned at him.

"Actually, I had another reason for wanting to get to know you – and if this hadn't happened, sooner or later I suppose I'd

32

have managed it somehow. I'm wild to know all about space travel and the stars! And I've never had a chance to learn anything about it! Tell me – how do the Big Ships find their way between stars? What moves the ships? Do the Terrans really have colonies on hundreds of worlds?"

"One question at a time!" Larry laughed, "and remember I'm only learning!" But he began to explain navigation to Kennard who listened, fascinated, asking question after question about the spaceships and the stars.

He was describing his one view of the drive rooms on the starship when the door swung open and a very tall man came in. Like Kennard, he had red hair, graying a little at the temples; his eyes were deepset, hawk-keen and stern, and he looked upright, handsome and immensely dignified in his scarlet embroidered jacket. Kennard got quickly to his feet, and Larry got up, too.

"So this is your friend, Kennard?" The man made a formal bow to Larry. "Welcome to our home, my boy. Kennard tells me you are a brave fellow, and have won the freedom of the city. Please consider yourself free of our house as well, at any time. I am Valdir Alton."

"Larry Montray, *z'par servu*," said Larry, bowing as he had seen Kennard do and using the most respectful Darkovan phrase, "At your service, sir."

"You lend us grace." The man smiled and took his hand. "I hope you will come to us often."

"I would like that very much, sir."

"You speak excellent Darkovan. It is rare to find one of your people who will do us even the small courtesy of learning our language so well," Valdir Alton said.

Larry felt inclined to protest. "My father speaks it even better than I do, sir."

"Then he is wise," Valdir replied.

"Father," Kennard cut in, excitedly; he might be a poised young soldier in the streets, but here, Larry saw, he was just a kid like Larry himself. "Father, Larry has promised to lend me some books about space travel and about the Empire! And, to get permission, if he can, to show me over the spaceport!"

"For that last, of course, you must not be disappointed if permission is refused," Valdir warned the boys, smiling indulgently. "They might think that you were a spy. But the books will be welcome; I myself shall enjoy seeing them. I can read a little of the Terran Standard language."

"I thought about that," Larry said. "I wasn't sure if Kennard could. These are mostly pictures and photographs."

"Thanks," Kennard laughed. "I *can* read our scripts if I have to – well enough for duty lists and the like – but I'm too busy for a scholar's work! Oh, I can write my name well enough to serve, but why should I spoil my eyes for the hunt by learning what any public scribe can do for me? If it's a question of pictures, though – that's something worth seeing!"

Larry, too startled to wonder whether it was polite, blurted out, "You can't even read your own language? Why, I can read Darkovan!"

"You *can*?" Kennard sounded honestly awed. "Why, I thought you weren't even old enough to bear arms – and you read two languages and can write too! Are you a scholar by trade, then?"

Larry shook his head.

"But how old are you? If you can read already?"

"I was sixteen three months ago."

"I'll be sixteen in the Dark Month," Kennard said. "I thought you were younger."

Valdir Alton, idly eating sweets from one of the bowls, interrupted, saying, "I should be sorry to fail in hospitality, Lerrys" – he spoke Larry's name with an odd, Darkovan accent – "but it is late and your spaceport curfew will be enforced. I think, Kennard, you must have your guest escorted home – unless you would like to spend the night? We have ample room for guests, and you would be welcome."

"Thank you, sir, but I'd better not. My father would worry, I'm afraid. If someone can tell me the way – "

"My bodyguards will take you," Kennard said, "but come again very soon. I'm on duty tomorrow and the next day, but – the day after? Could you come and spend the afternoon?"

"I'd like to," Larry promised.

"You had better wear those clothes," Valdir said; "your own, I fear, are fit only to clean floors. These are outworn ones of Kennard's brother; you need not return them."

Kennard went to the door with him, repeating his cordial

urgings to come again, and Larry, escorted by the silent guard, found his way quickly to the spaceport. His mind still on his adventure, he was brought up with a shock when the spaceport guard stopped him with a sharp challenge.

"What do you think you're doing here at this time of night? Nobody admitted now but spaceport personnel!"

With a shock, Larry remembered his Darkovan clothing. He produced his identity card, and the guard stared. "What the deuce you doing in *that* rig, kid? And you're late; half an hour more and I'd have to put you on report for the Commandant. Don't you know it's not safe to go prowling around at night?" He caught sight of Larry's bruised and reddened knuckles, his slowly blackening left eye. "Holy Joe, you look like you'd found that out. I bet you catch it when your Dad sees you!"

Larry was beginning to be a little afraid of that, himself. Well, there was nothing to do but face it.

It had been worth it, whatever Dad said. Even worth a licking, if it turned out that way.

IV

It was worse than he had thought it would be.

As he came through the doors of the apartment in Quarters A, he saw his father, intercom in hand, and heard Wade Montray's sharp, preoccupied voice, with overtones of trouble.

" – went out after school, and hasn't come in; I checked with all his friends. The guard at the western gate saw him leave, but hasn't seen him come back . . . I don't want to sound like an alarmist, sir, but if he'd wandered into the Old Town – you know as well as I do what could have happened. Yes, I know that, sir, and I'll take all the responsibility for letting it happen; it was foolish of me. Believe me, I realize that now – "

Larry said hesitantly "Dad – ?"

Montray started, half dropping the cap of the intercom.

"Larry! Is that you?"

Montray said into the intercom, "Forget it. He just came in. Yes, I know, I'll attend to it . . . All right, Larry, come in here where I can get a good look at you."

Larry obeyed, bracing himself for a storm. As he came into the main room, and the light fell on his bruised face, Montray turned pale.

"Larry, your face! Son, what's happened? Are you all right?" He came forward, quickly, taking Larry by the shoulders and turning him toward the light; Larry tensed, trying to pull away.

"It's all right, Dad; I got into a fight. A bunch of toughs. It's all right." He added quickly, "It looks worse than it is."

Montray's face worked, and for a moment he turned away. When he looked at Larry again, his face was controlled and grim, his voice level. "You'd better tell me about it."

Larry began the story, trying to make light of the roughing

36

up he had had, but his father interrupted, harshly, "You could have been killed! You know that, don't you?"

"I wasn't, though. And really, Dad, it's an incredible piece of luck, meeting Kennard and everything. It was worth a little trouble – Dad, what's wrong, what is it?"

Montray said, "I made a mistake ever letting you go into the town alone. I know that, now. That's all over. It could have been very serious. Larry, this is an order: You are not to leave the Terran Zone again – not at any time, not under any conditions,.."

Startled, outraged, hardly believing, Larry stared at his father. "You can't mean that, Dad!"

"But I do mean it."

"But you haven't even been listening to me, then! Nothing like that would happen again! Kennard said I had the freedom of the city, and his father invited me to come again – "

"I heard you perfectly well," his father cut in, "but you've had your orders, Larry, and I don't intend to discuss it any further. You are not to leave the Terran Zone again – at any time. No" – he raised his hand as Larry began to protest – "not another word, not one. Go and wash your face and put something on those cuts and get to bed. Get going!"

Larry opened his mouth and, slowly, shut it again. It wasn't the slightest use; his father wasn't listening to him. Fuming, outraged, he stalked toward his room.

It wasn't like Dad to treat him this way – like a little kid to be ordered around! Usually, Dad was reasonable. While he washed his bruised face and painted his skinned knuckles with antiseptic, he stormed silently inside. Dad *couldn't* mean it – not now, not after the trouble he'd had getting accepted!

Finally he decided to let it ride until morning. Dad had been worried about him; maybe when he'd had a chance to think it over, he'd listen to reason. Larry went to bed, still thinking over, with excitement, the new friend he'd made and the opportunity this opened up – the chance to see the real Darkover, not the world of the spaceport and the tourists but the strange, highly colored world that lay alien and beautiful beyond them.

Dad would *have* to see it his way!

But he didn't. When Larry tackled him again, over the

breakfast table, Montray's face was dark and forbidding, and would have intimidated anyone less determined than Larry.

"I said I didn't even want to discuss it. You've had your orders, and that's all there is to it."

Larry bit his lip, scowling furiously into his plate. Finally, flaming with indignation, he raised his head and stared defiantly at his father.

"I'm not taking that, sir."

Montray frowned again. "What did you say?"

Larry felt a queer, uneasy sensation under his belt. He had never openly defied his father since he was a toddler of four or five. But he persisted.

"Dad, I don't want to be disrespectful, but you can't treat me that way. I'm not a kid, and when you say something like that, I have a right, at least, to an explanation."

"You'll do as you're told, or else you'll – " Montray checked himself. At last he laid down his fork and leaned forward, his chin on his hands, his eyes angry. But all he said was, "Fair enough, then. Here's the story. Suppose, last night, you'd been badly hurt, or killed?"

"But I – "

"Let me finish. One silly kid goes exploring, and it could create an interplanetary incident. If you'd gotten into real trouble, Larry, we would have had to use all the power and prestige of the Terran Empire just to get you out of it again. If we had to do that – especially if we had to use force and Terran weapons – we'd lose all the good will and tolerance that it's taken us years to build up. It would all have to be done over again. Sure, if it came to a fight, we'd win. But we want to *avoid* incidents, not win fights which cost us more than we gain by winning them. Do you honestly think it's worth it?"

Larry hesitated.

"Well, do you?"

"I suppose not, when you put it that way," Larry said slowly. Mentally he was comparing this with what Kennard had said: how the Darkovans resented the use of the whole power of Terra, just to "pry into" what should be a private quarrel between one troublemaker and the people he had offended. It would also mean that if Larry had been harmed, the Terrans would have held all of Darkover responsible, not

38

just the few young toughs who had actually committed the incident.

He was trying to think how he could explain this to his father, but Montray left him no time. "That's the situation. No more exploring on your own. And no arguments, if you don't mind; I don't intend to discuss it any further with you. That's just the way it's got to be." He pushed away his plate and stood up. "I've got work to do."

Larry sat on at the empty breakfast table, a dull and simmering resentment burning through him. So Kennard had been right, after all. It seemed that all of Darkover and all of the Terran Empire had to be dragged into it.

His head throbbed and he could hardly see out of his black eye, and his knuckles were so swollen that he found it hard to handle a fork. He decided not to go to school, and spent most of the morning lying on his bed, bitterly resentful. This meant the end of his adventure. What else was there? The dull world of Quarters and spaceport, identical with the world he'd left on Earth. He might as well have stayed there!

He got out the books he had promised Kennard. So he couldn't even keep that promise! And Kennard would think his word wasn't worth anything. How could he get word to his Darkovan friend about the punishment imposed on him? Kennard, and Kennard's father, had shown him friendship and hospitality – and he couldn't even keep his word!

Well, they'd started out by not thinking much of the Terrans – and now their opinion would just be confirmed that Terrans weren't to be trusted.

The day dragged by. The next day he went back to school, turning aside queries about his black eye with some offhand story of falling over a chair in the darkness. But the day after, as the hour approached when he had promised the Altons to visit them his conflict grew and grew.

Damn it, he'd *promised*.

His father, looking into his glowering face at breakfast, had said briefly, "I'm sorry, Larry. This isn't pleasant for me – to deny you something you want so much. Some day, when you're older, perhaps you'll understand why I have to do this. Until then, I'm afraid you'll just have to accept my judgment."

He thinks he'll cut off my interest in Darkover just by forbidding me to go outside the Terran Zone, Larry thought resentfully. *He doesn't know anything about it, really – or about me!*

The day wore away, slowly. He considered, and rejected, the idea of a final appeal to his father. Wade Montray seldom gave an order, but when he did, he never rescinded it, and Larry could tell his father's mind was made up on this subject.

But it wasn't fair – and it wasn't right, or just! Painfully, Larry faced a decision that all youngsters face sooner or later: the knowledge that their parents are not always right – that sometimes they can be dead wrong!

Wrong or not, he thinks I ought to have to obey him anyhow! And that's the bad thing. What else can I do?

He thought that would have to be the end of it, but the question somehow stuck, uncomfortably, with him: Well, what else *can* I do?

I can refuse to obey him, the thought came suddenly, as if he had never had it before.

He had never deliberately defied his father. The thought made him uncomfortable.

But this time, I'm right and he's wrong, and if he can't see it, I can. I made a commitment, and if I break my word, that in itself is going to make a couple of Darkovans – and important people – think that Terrans aren't worth much.

This is one time where I'm going to *have* to disobey Dad. Afterwards, I'll take any punishment he wants to hand out to me. But I'm not going to break my word to Kennard and his father. I'll explain to them why I may not be able to come again, but I won't insult their hospitality by just disappearing and not even letting them know why I never came back.

Kennard saved me from a mauling – maybe from being killed. I promised him something he wants – some books – and I owe him that much.

He was uneasy about disobeying. But he still felt, deep down, that he was right.

If I'd been born on Darkover, he told himself, I'd be considered a man; old enough to do a man's work, old enough to make my own decisions – and take the consequences. There comes a time in your life when you have to decide for yourself what is right and what is wrong, and stop accepting what older people say. Dad may be right as far as he knows, but he doesn't know the whole story, and I do. And I've got to do what I think is right.

He wondered why he felt so sad about it. It hurt, suddenly, to realize that he'd made a decision he could never go back on. He might be punished like a child, when he got back; but suddenly he understood that he'd never feel like one again. It wasn't just the act of disobeying his father – any kid could do that. It was that he had decided, once and for all, that he no longer was *willing* to let his father decide right and wrong for him. If he obeyed his father, after this, it would be because he had thought it over and decided, on a grown-up basis, that he wanted to obey him.

And it hurt. He felt a funny pain about it, but it never occurred to him to change his mind. He'd decided what he was going to do. Now he had to decide how he was going to do it.

His father had mentioned that if he, Larry, got into trouble, it might drag the whole Terran Zone into it. That was something to consider. That was fair enough. Larry wanted to be sure there was no danger of that.

Then he thought: *I could be taken for a Darkovan, except for my clothes. I have been mistaken for a Darkovan by my accent. If I'm not dressed as a Terran, then I won't get into any trouble.*

And, he added to himself rather grimly, *if anything does happen to me, the Terrans won't be dragged into it. It will be my own responsibility.*

Quickly, he got out of his own clothes and put on the Darkovan ones Kennard had lent him. He glanced briefly at himself in the mirror. Part of himself recognized, a little ironic awareness, that he was enjoying the masquerade. It was exciting, an adventure. The other half of his awareness was a little grim. By deliberately taking off everything that could identify himself as a Terran, he was deliberately giving up his right to the protection of the Empire. Now he was on his own. He'd walk down into the city with no more protection than his two hands and his knowledge of the language could give him.

As if I were really Darkovan born, and entirely on my own!

41

He had halfway anticipated being stopped at the gate, but he passed through the archway without challenge, and went out into the city.

It was the hour when workmen were returning home, and the streets were crowded. He walked through them without attracting a glance, a strange breathless excitement growing under his ribs, and bursting in him. With every step, he seemed somehow to leave the person he had been, further behind. It was as if his present dress was not a masquerade, but rather as if he had simply discovered a deeper layer of himself, and was living with it. The pale cold sun hung high in the sky, casting purple shadows across the narrow streets and alleys; he found his way through the outlying reaches of the city with the instinct of a cat. He was almost sorry when he finally reached the distant quarter where the house of the Altons lay.

The nonhuman he had seen before opened the door for him, but Kennard was standing in the hallway, and Larry wondered briefly if the Darkovan boy had been waiting for him.

"You did make it," Kennard said, with a grin of satisfaction. "Somehow I'd had the feeling you wouldn't be able to, but when I looked this afternoon, I realized you would."

The words were confusing; Larry tried to make sense of them, finally decided that they must be some Darkovan idiom he didn't understand too well. He said, "I thought, for a while, that I couldn't come," but he left it at that.

The nonhuman moved toward him, and Larry flinched and drew away involuntarily, remembering his encounter with one in the streets. Kennard said quickly, "Don't be afraid of the *kyrri*. It's true that if strangers brush against them they give off sparks, but he won't hurt you now he knows you. They've been servants to our families for generations."

Larry allowed the nonhuman to take his cloak, looking curiously at the creature. It was erect and vaguely manlike, but covered with a pelt of long grayish fur, and it had long prehensile fingers and a face like a masked monkey. He wondered where the *kyrri* came from and what sort of curious relationships could exist between human and nonhuman. Would he ever know?

"I brought you the books I promised," he told Kennard, and the other boy took them eagerly. "Oh, good! But I'll look at them later. We needn't stand here in the hall. Do you know how to play darts? Shall we have a game?"

Larry agreed with interest. Kennard showed him the game in a big downstairs room, wide and light, with translucent walls, evidently a game-room of some sort. The darts were light and perfectly balanced, feathered with crimson and green feathers from some exotic bird. Once Larry grew accustomed to their weight and balance, he found that they were well matched in the game. But they played it desultorily, Kennard breaking off now and again to leaf through the books, stare fascinated at the many photographs, and ask endless questions about star-travel.

They were in one such lull in the game when the curtained panels closing off the room swirled back and Valdir Alton came in, followed by another man – a tall Darkovan, with copper hair sweeping back from a high stern forehead marked with two wings of white hair. He wore an embroidered cloak of a curious cut. The boys broke off in their game, and Kennard, with a start of surprise, made the stranger a deep and formal bow. The newcomer glanced sharply at Larry, and, not wishing to seem rude, Larry repeated the gesture.

The man spoke some offhand phrase of polite acknowledgment, nodding pleasantly to both boys; but as his gray gaze crossed Larry's, he started, narrowed his brows, then turning his head to Valdir, said, "Terran?"

Valdir did not speak, but they looked at one another for a moment. The stranger nodded, crossed the room and stood in front of Larry. Slowly, as if compelled, Larry looked up at him, unable to draw his eyes away from his intense and compelling stare. He felt as if he were being weighed in the balance, sorted out, drawn out; as if the old man's searching look went down beneath his borrowed clothes, down to the alien bones under his flesh, down to his deepest thoughts and memories. It was like being hypnotized. He found himself suddenly shivering, and then, suddenly, he could look away again, and the man was smiling down at him, and the strange gray eyes were kind.

He said to Valdir, speaking past the boys, "So this is why you brought me here, Valdir? Don't worry; I have sons of my own. Introduce me to your friend, Kennard."

43

Kennard said "The lord Lorill Hastur, one of the elders of the Council."

Larry had heard the name from his father, spoken with exasperation but a certain degree of respect. He thought, *I hope my being here doesn't mean trouble, after all,* and for a brief instant almost regretted coming; then let it pass. The tension in the room slackened indefinably. Valdir picked up one of the books Larry had brought Kennard, turning the pages with interest; Lorill Hastur came and looked over his shoulder, then turned away and began examining the darts. He drew back his arm and tossed one accurately into the target. Valdir put the book down and looked up at Larry.

"I was sure that you would be able to come today."

"I wanted to. But I may not be able to come again," Larry said.

Valdir's eyes were narrowed, curious: "Too dangerous?"

"No," said Larry, "that doesn't bother me. It's that my father would rather I didn't." He stopped; he didn't want to discuss his father, or seem to complain about his father's unreasonableness. That was something between his father and himself, not to be shared with outsiders. The conflict touched him again with sadness. He liked Kennard so much better than any of the friends he had made in Quarters, and yet this friendship must be given up almost before it had a chance to be explored. He took up one of the darts and turned it, end for end, in his hand; then flung it at the target board, missing his aim. Lorill Hastur turned and faced him again.

"How is it that you were willing to risk trouble and even punishment to come today, Larry?"

It did not occur to Larry to wonder – not until much later – how the Elder had known his name, or the inner conflict that had forced a choice on him. Just then it seemed natural that this old man with the searching eyes knew everything about him. But he still wasn't ready to sound disloyal.

"I didn't have a chance to make him understand. He would have realized why I had to come."

"And breaking your word would have been an insult," Lorill Hastur said gravely. "It is part of the code of a man to make his own choices."

He smiled at the boys, and turned, without formal leave-taking. Valdir took a step to follow him, turned back to Larry.

"You are welcome here at any time."

"Thank you, sir. But I'm afraid I won't be able to come again. Not that I wouldn't like to."

Valdir smiled. "I respect your choice. But I have a feeling we'll meet again." He followed Lorill Hastur out of the room.

Alone with Kennard, Larry found room for wonder. "How did he know so much about me?"

"The Hastur-Lord? He's a telepath, of course. What else?" Kennard said, matter-of-factly, his face buried in a book of views taken in deep space. "What sort of camera do they use for this? I never have been able to understand how a camera works."

And Larry, explaining the principle of sensitized film to Kennard, felt an amused, ironic surprise. *Telepath, of course!* And to Kennard this was the commonplace and something like a camera was exotic and strange. It was all in the point of view.

Far too soon, the declining sun told him it was time to go. He refused Kennard's urgings to stay longer. He did not want his father to be frightened at his absence. Also, at the back of his mind, was a memory like a threat – if he was missing, might his father set the machinery of the Terran Empire into motion to locate him, bring down trouble on his friends? Kennard went a little way with him, and at the corner of the street paused, looking at him rather sadly.

"I don't like to say goodbye, Larry," he said. "I like you. I wish – "

Larry nodded, a little embarrassed, but sharing the emotion. "Maybe we'll see each other again," he said, and held out his hand. Kennard hesitated, long enough for Larry to feel first offended, then worried for fear he had committed some breach of Darkovan manners; then, deliberately, the Darkovan boy reached both hands and took Larry's between them. Larry did not know for years how rare a gesture this was in the Darkovan caste to which the Altons belonged. Kennard said softly, "I won't say good-bye. Just – good luck."

45

He turned swiftly and walked away without looking back.

Larry turned his steps toward home, in the lowering mist. As he moved between the dark canyons of the streets, his feet steadying themselves automatically on the uneven stones, he felt a flat undefined sorrow, as if he were seeing all this with the poignancy of a farewell. It was as if life had opened a bright door, and then slammed it again, leaving the world duller by contrast.

Suddenly, his feeling of sadness thinned out and vanished. This was only a temporary thing. He wouldn't be a kid forever. The time would come when he'd be free and on his own, free to explore all the worlds of his own choosing – and Darkover was only one of many. He had tasted a man's freedom today – and some day it would be his for all time.

His head went up and he crossed the square toward the spaceport, steadily. He'd had his fun, and he could take whatever happened. It had been worth it.

He had the curious sense that he was re-living something that had happened before, as he entered their apartment in the Quarters building. His father was waiting for him, his face drawn, unreadable.

"Where have you been?"

"In the city. At the home of Kennard Alton."

Montray's face contracted with anger, but his voice was level and stern.

"You do remember that I forbade you to leave the Terran Zone? You're not going to tell me that you forgot?"

"I didn't forget."

"In other words, you deliberately disobeyed."

Larry said quietly, "Yes."

Montray was evidently holding his anger in check with some effort. "Precisely why, when I did forbid it?"

Larry paused a moment before answering. Was he simply making excuses about having done what he wanted to do? Then he was sure, again, of the rightness of his position.

"Because, Dad, I'd made a promise and I didn't feel it was right to break it, without a better reason than just that you'd forbidden it. This was something *I* had to do, and you were treating me like a kid. I tried to make sure that you wouldn't

46

be involved, or the Terran Empire, if anything had happened to me."

His father said, at last, "And you felt you should make that decision for yourself. Very well, Larry, I admire your honesty. Just the same, I refuse to concede that you have a right to ignore my orders on principle. You know I don't like punishing you. However, for the present you will consider yourself under house arrest – not to leave our quarters except to go to school, under any pretext." He paused and a bleak smile touched his lips. "Will you obey me, or shall I inform the guards not to let you pass without reporting it?"

Larry flinched at the severity of the punishment, but it was just. From his father's point of view, it was the only thing he could do. He nodded, not looking up.

"Anything you say, Dad. You've got my word."

Montray said, without sarcasm. "You have shown me that it means something to you. I'll trust you. House arrest until I decide you can be trusted with your freedom again."

The next days dragged slowly by, no day distinguishing itself from the last. The bruises on his face and hands healed, and his Darkovan adventure began to seem dim and pallid, as if it had happened a long time ago. Nevertheless, even in the dullness of his punishment, which deprived him even of things he had previously not valued – freedom to go about the spaceport and the Terran city, to visit friends and shops – he never doubted that he had done the right thing. He chafed under the restriction, but did not really regret having earned it.

Ten days had gone by, and he was beginning to wonder a little when his father would see fit to lift the sentence, when the order came from the Commandant.

His father had just come in, one evening, when the intercom buzzed, and when Montray put the phone down, he looked angry and apprehensive.

"Your idiotic prank is probably coming home to roost," he said angrily. "That was the Legate's office in Administration. You and I have both been ordered to report there this evening – and it was a priority summons."

"Dad, if it means trouble for you, I'm sorry. You'll have to tell them you forbade me to go – and if you don't, I will. I'll take all the blame myself." For the first time, Larry felt that the consquences might really go beyond himself. *But that's not my fault – it's because the administration is unreasonable. Why should Dad be blamed for what I did?*

He had never been in the administration building before, and as he approached the great white skyscraper that loomed over the whole spaceport complex, he was intrigued to the point of forgetting that he was here for a reproof. The immense building, glimmering with white metal and glass, the wide halls and the panoramic view from each corridor window of the Darkovan city below and the mountains beyond, almost took his breath away. The Legate's office was high up, bright and filled with lowering red sunshine; for a moment, as he stepped into the brilliant glassed-in room, a curious thought flashed through Larry's mind: *He sees more of this world than he wants anyone to know about.*

The Legate was a stocky man, dark and grizzled, with thoughtful eyes and a permanent frown. Nevertheless, he had dignity, and something which made Larry think quickly of Lorill Hastur. *What is it? Is it just that they're used to power, or to making decisions that other people have to live with?*

"Commander Reade – my son Larry."

"Sit down." It was a peremptory command, not an invitation. "So you've been roaming around in the city? Tell me about it – tell me everything you've done there."

His face was unreadable; without anger, but without friendliness. Reserving judgment. Neither kind nor unkind. But there was immense authority in it, as if he expected Larry to jump at once to obey him; and after ten days of sulking in Quarters, Larry wasn't feeling especially humble.

"I didn't know it was against any rules, sir. And I didn't hurt anyone, and nothing happened to me."

Reade made a noncommittal sound. "Suppose you let me decide about that. Just tell me about it."

Larry told the whole story: his wanderings in the city day after day, his meeting with the gang of toughs, and the intervention of Kennard Alton. Finally he told of his last visit to the Alton house, making it clear that he had gone without his father's knowledge and consent. "So don't blame Dad, sir. *He* didn't break any laws, at least."

Montray said quickly, "Just the same, Reade, I'll take the

48

responsibility. He's my son, and I'll be responsible for his not doing it again."

Reade gestured him to silence. "That's not the problem. "We've heard from the Council – on behalf of the Altons. It seems that they are deeply and gravely offended."

"What? Why?"

"Because you have refused your son permission to pursue this friendship – they say you have insulted them, as if they were unfit to associate with your son."

Montray put his hands to his temples, wearily. He said, "Oh, my God."

"Exactly," Reade said in a soft voice. "The Altons are important people on Darkover – aristocrats, members of the Council. A snub or slight from a Terran can create trouble."

Suddenly his voice exploded in wrath. "Confound the boy anyhow! We aren't ready for this sort of episode. We should have thought of it ourselves and made preparation for it, and now when it hits us, we can hardly make good use of it! How old is the boy?"

Montray gestured at Larry to answer for himself, and Reade grunted. "Sixteen, huh? Here they're men at that age – and we ought to realize it! What about it, young Larry? Are you intending – have you ever considered going into the Empire service?"

Puzzled by the question, Larry said, "I've always intended that, Commander."

"Well, here's your chance." He tossed a small squarish slip of paper across the table. It was thick and bordered, and had Darkovan writing on it, the straight squarish script of the city language. He said, "I understand you can read some of this stuff. God knows why you bothered, but it makes it handy for us. Figure it out later when you get the chance; as it happens, I can read it too, though most people in Administration *don't* bother. It's an invitation from the Altons – coming through Administration as a slap in the face: they don't like the way Terrans tend to go through channels on every little thing – for you, Larry, to spend the next season at their country estate, with Kennard."

Montray's face went dark as if a shutter had dropped over

his eyes. "Impossible, Reade. I know what you have in mind, and I won't go along with it."

Reade's face did not change. "You see the position this puts us in. The boy's not prepared for the tremendous opportunity this opens up, but we've still got to grab this chance. We simply can't afford to let Larry refuse this invitation. For God's sake, do you realize that we've been trying to get permission for someone to visit the outlying estates, for fifteen years? It's the first time in years that any Terran has had this chance, and if we turn it down, it may be years before it comes again."

Montray's mouth twisted. "Oh, there have been a few."

"Yes, I know." Reade did not elaborate, but turned to Larry. "Do you understand why you're going to have to accept this invitation?"

Suddenly, with the visual force of a hallucination, Larry saw again the tall figure of Valdir Alton, and heard him say, as clearly as if he had been in that white Terran room with them, *I have a feeling we'll see you again before long.* It was so real that he shook his head to clear it of the abnormally intense impression.

Reade persisted. "You *are* going to accept?"

Larry felt a delayed surge of excitement. To see Darkover – not only the city, but far outside the Terran Zone entirely, the real world, untouched by Terra! The thought was a little frightening and yet wildly exciting. But a tinge of caution remained and he said warily. "Would you mind telling me why you are so eager to have me, sir? I understood that the Terrans were afraid of any – fraternization with Darkovans."

"Afraid of it causing trouble," Reade said. "We've been trying to arrange something like this, though, for years. I suppose they felt we were a little too eager, and were afraid we'd try something. Larry, I can explain it very easily. First of all, we don't want to offend Darkovan aristocrats. But more than that. This is the first time Darkovans of power and position have actually made an advance of personal friendliness to any Terran. They trade with us, they accept us here, but they don't want to have anything to do with us personally. This is like a breach in that wall. You have a unique opportunity to be – a sort of ambassador for Terra. Perhaps, to show them that we aren't anything to fear. And then, too – " He hesitated. "Very few Terrans have ever seen anything of this planet except what the Darkovans wanted us to see. You should keep very careful records of everything you see, because something you don't even realize is important might mean everything to us."

Larry saw through that at once.

"Are you asking me to *spy* on my friends?" he asked, in outrage.

"No, no," Reade said quickly, even though Larry felt very clearly that Reade was thinking that he was a little too clever. "Just to keep your eyes open and tell us what you see. Chances are they will be expecting you to do that anyhow."

Montray interrupted, pacing the floor restlessly, "I don't like having my son used as a pawn in power politics. Not by Darkovans trying to get next to us – and not by the Terran Empire trying to find out about Darkover, either!"

"You're exaggerating, Montray. Look, at least a few of the higher Darkovan caste may be telepaths; we couldn't plant the kid on them as a spy, even if we tried. It's just a chance to know a little more about them."

He appealed directly to Larry: "You say you liked this Darkovan youngster. Doesn't it make sense – to try and build friendly relations between the two of you?"

That thought had already crossed Larry's mind. He nodded. Montray said reluctantly, "I still don't like it. But there's nothing I can do."

Reade looked at him and Larry was shocked at the quick expression of triumph and power in the man's face. He thought, *He enjoys this*. He wondered, suddenly, why he could see into the man this way. He was sure he knew more about Commander Reade than Reade wanted him to know. Reade said softly over Larry's head to Wade Montray, "We've got to do it this way. Your son is old enough, and he's not scared – are you, Larry? So all we have to do is tell the Altons that he'll be proud and honored to visit them – and say when."

Back again in their apartment in Quarters A, Larry's father swore under his breath, ceaselessly, for almost a quarter of an hour. "And now you see what you've gotten yourself into," he finished at last, viciously. "Larry, I don't like it, I don't like it, I don't *like* it! And damn it, I suppose you're overjoyed – you've got what you want!''

Larry said, honestly, "It's interesting, Dad. But I am a little scared. Reade wants me to go for all the wrong reasons.''

'I'm glad you can see *that*, at least,'' Montray snapped. "I ought to let you hang yourself. You got yourself into this. Just the same – '' He grew silent; then he got up and came to his son, and took Larry by the shoulders again, looking very searchingly at him. His voice was gentler than Larry could remember hearing it in years.

"Listen, son. If you really don't want to get into this, I'll get you out of it, somehow. You're my son, not just a potential Empire employee. They can't force you to go. Don't worry about their putting pressure on me – I can always put in for a transfer somewhere else. I'll *leave* the damned planet before I let them force you to play their games!''

Larry, feeling his father's hands on his shoulders, suddenly realized that he was being given a chance – perhaps the last chance he would ever have – to return to the old, protected status of a child. He could be his father's son again, and Dad would get him out of this. So the step he had taken, in declaring himself a man, was not quite irrevocable after all. He could return to the safe age, and the price was very small. His father would take care of him.

He found himself wanting to, almost desperately. He'd bitten off more than he could chew, and this was his chance to get out of it. The alternative would put him on his own, in a strange world, playing a strange part, respresenting his Terran world all alone.

And the Altons would know that his man's decision had been a lie, that he clung to the safety of being a Terran child hiding behind his society –

He drew a long breath, and put his hands up over his father's.

"Thanks, Dad,'' he said, warmly, meaning it. "I almost wish I could take you up on that. Honestly. But I have to go. As you say, I got myself into this, and I might as well get some good out of it – for all of you. Don't worry, Dad – it's going to be all right.''

Montray's hands tightened on his shoulders. His eyes met

his son's, and he said. "I was afraid you'd feel that way, Larry – and I wish you didn't. But I guess, being who you are, you'd have to. I could still forbid you, I guess" – a wry smile flitted across his face – "but I've found out you're too old for that, and I won't even try." He dropped his hands, but then a wide grin spread across his worried face.

"Damn it, son – I still don't like it – but I'm proud of you."

V

The morning mist had burned off the hills, but still lay thick in the valley. Above the bank of pinkish cloud, the red sun hung in a bath of thinning mist. Larry looked down at the treetops emerging from the top of the cloud, and drew a deep breath, savoring the strange scents of the alien forest.

He rode last in the little column of six men. Ahead of him, Kennard looked round briefly, lifted a hand in acknowledgment of his grin, and turned back.

Larry had been at Armida, the outlying country estate of the Altons, for twelve days now. The journey from the city had been tiring; he was not accustomed to riding, and though at first it had been a pleasant novelty, he found himself thinking regretfully of the comfortable ground-cars and airships of Terran travel.

But the slow trip through forests and mountains had gradually won him to its charm: the high rocky trails reaching summits where crimson and purple landscapes lay rainbow-lovely below them, the deep shadowed roads through the forest, with here and there tall white towers rising high against the horizon, or glowing faintly luminescent in the night. At night they had either camped along the roadway, or now and again guests in some outlying farmhouse where the Darkovans had treated Valdir and Kennard with extreme deference – and Larry had come in for his own share of this respect. Valdir had told no one that his son's guest and companion was one of the alien Terrans.

The home of the Altons was a great gray rambling structure, too low for a castle, too imposing to be a house. He found himself fitting into the place easily, riding with Kennard, helping him train his hunting dogs, learning to shoot with the curiously shaped crossbows they used for sport, savoring

54

the strangeness of the life he lived. It was all very interesting, but certainly nothing that he could tell Reade which might be of benefit to the Terrans – and he was glad of it. He hadn't liked the idea of being what amounted to a spy.

Mostly the days were too full for much introspection, but sometimes when he was in bed at night, he found himself wondering why the invitation had been issued in the first place. He liked Kennard, they were friends, but would that alone cause Valdir Alton to ignore the long tradition on Darkover of ignoring the Terrans?

He found himself wondering if Valdir's reason for issuing the invitation were not very much the same as Reade's reason for wanting Larry to accept it – that Valdir just wanted to know something about the Terrans, close up.

He was, by now, used to riding, and a three-day hunt had been arranged partly for his benefit. He had managed to shoot well enough to bring down a small rabbitlike beast on the first day, which had been cooked over the campfire that evening, and he was proud of that, even though it was the only thing he had hit during the long hunt.

At the top of the hill he drew even with Kennard, and they sat breathing their horses, side by side, looking across the valley.

"It's nice up here," Kennard said at last. "I used to ride this way fairly often, a couple of seasons ago. Father feels that now it's too dangerous for me to come alone." He gestured at their escort, Darkovans Larry did not know: one a well-dressed young redhead from a nearby estate, the others men from Alton farms, workmen of various sorts. One was in the uniform of the Guards, but Kennard himself was wearing old riding-clothes, slightly too small for him.

"Dangerous? Why?"

"It's too near the edge of the forests," Kennard said, "and during the last few seasons, trailmen have spread down into these forests. Usually they stay in the hills. They're not really dangerous, but they don't like humans, and we stay out of their way, as a rule. Then, too, this is on the border of mountain country, and men from the Cahuengas – "

He broke off, stiffening in his saddle, looking intently across the valley.

"What is it, Kennard?" Larry asked.

The Darkovan boy pointed. Larry could see nothing, but Kennard called to his father, a shrill insistent shout, and Valdir turned his horse and came cantering back.

"What's wrong, Ken?"

"Smoke. The mist lifted just for a minute, over there – " Kennard pointed, "and I saw it. Right at the edge of the Ranger station."

Valdir frowned, narrowing his eyes, shading them with his thin brown hand. "How sure are you? It's a good hour's ride out of our way – damn this mist, I can't see anything." He flung back his head like a deer sniffing the wind, peering into the distance, and finally nodded.

"A trace of smoke. We'll ride and check." He glanced at Larry. "I hope you don't mind the extra riding."

"Not at all, but I hope nothing's wrong, Lord Alton."

"So do I," Valdir said, his brows drawn down with worry, and touched his horse's flank with a light heel. They were off down the trail, the sound of hoofs making a dull clamor on the leaves underfoot. As they neared the bottom of the valley, the mist lifted slightly and the men pointed and shouted. Larry's nostrils twitched at a faint, acrid whiff of strange smoke. The sun had swung southward, and they were turning their horses up a widened trail that led to the top of a little hill, when Valdir Alton let out a great curse, rising in his stirrups and pointing; then he clapped his heels to his horse's side and vanished over the top of the rise. Kennard spurred after him, and Larry, urging his horse forward, felt a surge of excitement and fear as he followed. He came over the rise in the road and heard Kennard cry out in consternation; he pulled up his horse and looked down, in dismay, at a grove of trees from which black smoke was coiling upward.

Kennard slid from his horse and began to run. The man in the Guardsman's uniform called to him and drew his crossbow up to rest, and Larry realized, with a shiver, that they were all looking warily at the surrounding trees. What might lie behind them?

Valdir leaped from his saddle; the other men followed suit,

and Larry slid down with the rest. The deathly silence seemed more ominous because it was cut through with the soft chirping of birds from a distance, twittering in the grove.

Then Kennard called; he was kneeling in the road beside what Larry thught to be a gray boulder, but he put out his hand to turn it and Larry, his stomach cramping in horror, saw that it was the hunched body of a man in a gray cloak.

Valdir bent over the man; straightened. Larry stood frozen, looking down at death. He had never seen a dead body before, let alone the body of a man dead by violence. The dead man was young, little more than a boy, a shadow of thin beard on his face. A great wound in his chest gaped black and bloody. He had been dead some time.

Kennard was looking pale. Larry turned away, feeling faint and sick, and struggling not to show it, as Valdir turned away from the dead man.

"Cahuenga – his cloak is Cahuenga from the far hills," he said, "but boots and belt are from Hyalis. A raider – but no beacon flared when this station was attacked." He stepped warily around the corpse. The Guardsman shouted. "Don't go up there alone, Lord Alton!" and, sliding from his saddle, crossbow lowered, ran to follow him. Kennard followed, and Larry, as if compelled, ran after them.

A blackened ruin, still smoking, showed the vague outline of a building. On a little stretch of green at one side lay the crumpled body of a man. When Kennard and Larry reached Valdir's side, Valdir was already kneeling beside the body. After one glance, Larry turned away from the glazed, pain-ridden eyes; the man was bleeding from a great gash across his side, and from his lips a little dark-flecked foam stirred with his rasping breath.

Over the inert body the other Darkovan aristocrat looked at Valdir; gripped the limp wrist. His forehead was ridged with dismay. Valdir, looking up, said, "He must speak before he dies, Rannirl. And he's dying anyway."

Rannirl's mouth was set. He nodded, fumbled at his belt, and from a leather wallet drew forth a small, blue-glazed vial stoppered with silver. Handling it carefully, and keeping his own face free of the small fumes that coiled up from the open mouth of the vial, he measured a few cautious drops in the

57

cap; Valdir forced the man's mouth open and Rannirl let the fuming liquid fall on the man's tongue. After a moment a great shudder ran through the frame of the dying man, and the eyes fluttered.

His voice sounded harsh, far away. "*Vai dom* – we did what we could – the beacon – fire – "

Valdir gripped the limp hands, his face terrible and intent. There was something in his hands, something that glittered cold and blue; he pressed it to the dying man's forehead, and Larry saw that it was a clear blue jewel. Valdir said, "Do not spend your strength in speaking, Garin, or you will die before I learn what I must know. Form your thought clearly while you can, and I will understand. And forgive me, friend. You may save many lives with this torment." He bent close to the dying face, his own features a grim mask, lighted blue as the strange jewel suddenly flared and burned as if with inner flame. A spasm of terrible anguish passed over the dying Ranger's face; he shuddered twice and lay still, and Valdir, with a painful sigh, released his hands and straightened up. His own forehead was beaded with sweat; he swayed, and Kennard leaped to steady his father.

After a minute Valdir passed his hand over his wet brow, and spoke: "They didn't sell their lives cheaply," he said. "There were a dozen men; they came from the North, and hacked Balhar to pieces while he was trying to reach the beacon and set it aflame. He thought at first that they were Cahuenga, but two were tall pale men who were hooded almost like the *kyrri*, and one was masked. He saw them signal; they carried a mirror-flash device of some sort. After he fell, Garin saw them ride away northward toward the Kardarin."

Rannirl whistled softly. "If they could spare so many to prevent one beacon being lighted – this doesn't look like a few bandits out after a raid on the farms in the valley!"

Valdir swore. "There aren't enough of us to go after them," he said, "and we've only hunting weapons. And Zandru alone knows what other devil's work has been done along here. Kennard" – he turned to his son – "go and light the beacon, at least. Quickly! Garin tried to crawl there, when they had left him for dead, but his strength failed – " His voice went thin in his throat; he bent and covered the dead face with the Ranger's cloak.

"He didn't fight me," he said. "Even for a man weakened with many wounds and after a dose of that devil's drug of your, Rannirl, that takes a rare kind of courage."

He sighed, then, recovering himself, told two of the workmen to bury the dead Rangers. The sound of mattock and pick rang dully in the grove; after a few minutes, Kennard came running back.

"No way to light the beacon, father. Those devils took the time to drench it with water, just in case!"

Valdir swore, again, moodily, biting his lip. "The people along the valley should be warned, and someone should track them and find which way. We can't go to all four winds at once!" He stood for a moment, scowling, thoughtful. "If we had enough men we might take them at the fords or if we could warn the countryside by beacon – "

Abruptly he seemed to come to a decision.

"There aren't enough of us to follow them, and they've too big a head start in any case. But his probably means a good-sized raid. We've got to warn the people in the valley – and we can find a tracker there who can get on their trail and follow it better than we could. Nothing's likely to happen before night." He glanced up at the sun, trembling crimson at the zenith. "The hunt's over; we'll eat a bit then start back. Kennard, you and Larry – " he hesitated. "I'd like to send you both back to Armida, but you can't cross this country by yourselves. You'll have to ride with us." He looked at Larry. "It may mean some hard riding, I'm afraid."

The men had finished burying the Rangers; Valdir vetoed making a cookfire, directing the men to get cold food from their saddlebags. They sat eating, grimly discussing the burnt station and the dead Rangers in a dialect of which Larry could understand little. He could not eat; the food stuck in his throat. It was his first sight of violence and death and it had sickened him. He had known that violence was not unheard-of on Darkover, he had himself had a brief brush with it in his fight with the street boys, but now it assumed a dark and frightening aspect. With an almost painful nostalgia, he wished he were back in the safety of the Terran Zone.

59

Or was that safety, too, a mere illusion? Was there violence and cruelty and fear there, too, hidden behind the façades, and was he just now becoming aware of all these things? He choked over the piece of dry biscuit he was eating, and turned his eyes away from Kennard's too-searching gaze.

Valdir Alton's tall form shadowed him, and the Darkovan lord dropped on the grass at his side. He said, "Sorry that your hunt had to end this way, Lerrys. It wasn't what we planned."

"Do you really think I'd be worrying about a hunt when people are dead?" Larry asked.

Valdir's eyes were shrewd. "Nothing like this in your life before? Nothing like this in your world? Everything in the Terran Zone very neat and law-abiding?" Once again Larry had the feeling that – as with Lorill Hastur – his thoughts were being read. He remembered, with a small twinge of fear, how Valdir Alton had probed the mind of the dying Ranger.

He said, "I suppose there are law-breakers on Earth and in the Terran Zone, too. Only here it seems so – "

"So close up and personal?" Valdir asked. "Tell me something, Lerrys: Is a man more or less dead when he is killed neatly by a gun or a bomb, than when he is – " He moved his head toward where the dead Ranger had lain. His face was sudenly bitter as he added, "That seems to be the main difference between your people and ours. At least the men who killed poor Garin did not do their killing while they were a safe distance away!"

Larry said – glad to have something between himself and the memory of a dead man with a bleeding wound in his chest – "The main thing is that most of our people don't do any killing at all! We have laws and police to handle that sort of thing for us!"

"While here we feel that every man should handle his own affairs for himself, before they spread into wars," Valdir said steadily. "If any man offends me, damages my property or my family, steals my goods – it's my personal duty to revenge myself on that man – or to forgive him, if I see fit, without dragging in others who really have no part in the quarrel."

Larry was trying to fit that together – the contrast between the fierce individualism of the Darkovan code, and the Terran's acceptance of an orderly society, based on rules and laws. "A government of laws and not of men," he said, and at Valdir's raised eyebrow, explained, "that's supposed to be the original theory behind the Terran governments."

"While ours is a government of men – because laws can't be anything but the expression of men who make them," Valdir said. His face was grave and serious and Larry knew that while he might have started this conversation for the purpose of taking his young guest's mind off the scene of unfamiliar violence, now he was deeply involved in what he was saying. "It's one reason we want little to do with the Terrans, as such," he said. "Without offense to you personally. It's true that we have wars on Darkover, but they are small local hand-to-hand skirmishes; they seldom get bigger than this – " again he motioned towards the blackening ruin of the Ranger station. "The individual who makes trouble is promptly punished and the matter ends there, without involving a whole countryside."

"But – " Larry hesitated, remembering he was Valdir's guest. The older man said encouragingly, "Go ahead."

"Kennard has told me something of this, sir. You have long-lived feuds and when a troublemaker is punished, his family takes revenge, and doesn't this lead to more and more trouble over the years? Your way doesn't really *settle* anything. Really lawless people – like these bandits – ought to be dealt with by the law, shouldn't they?"

"You're entirely too clever," Valdir said, with a bleak smile. "That's the one flaw in the system. We use their own methods to revenge ourselves on them; they raid us, we raid them back, and we're as bad as they are. Actually, Larry, it goes deeper than that. Darkover seems to be in one of those uncomfortable times to live in – a time of change. And having the Terrans here hasn't helped. Again – without offense to you personally – having a highly technical civilization among us makes our people dissatisfied. We live the way men were meant to live – in close contact with real things, not huddled in cities and factories." He looked around, past the burnt station, at the high mountains, and said, "Can't you see it, Larry?"

"I can see it," Larry admitted, but a brief stab of doubt struck at him. When he had said the same thing, his own father had accused him of being a romantic. The Darkovans seemed to want to go on living as if change did not exist, and whether they liked it or not, the space age was here – and they *had* chosen to let the Terran Empire come here for trade.

"Yes," Valdir said, reading his thoughts. "I can see that too – change is coming, whether we like it or not. And I want it to come in an orderly fashion, without upheaval. Which means I've made myself awfully damned unpopular with a lot of people in my own caste. For instance, I organized this defense system of border stations and Rangers, so that every farm and estate wouldn't have to stand alone against raids by bandits from across the Kadarin. And there are some people who find this a clear violation of our code of individual responsibility." He stopped. "What's the matter?"

Larry blurted out, "You're reading my mind!"

"Does that bother you? I don't pry, Larry. No telepath does. But when you're throwing your thoughts at me so clearly – " he shrugged. "I've never known a Terran to be so open to rapport."

"No," Larry said, "it doesn't bother me." To his own surprise, that was true. He found that the idea didn't bother him at all. "Maybe if more Terrans and Darkovans could read each other's minds they'd understand one another better, and not be afraid of each other, any more than you and I are afraid of each other."

Valdir smiled at him kindly and stood up. "Time to get on the road again," he said; then breaking off, added very softly, "But don't deceive yourself, Larry. We are afraid of you. You don't know, yourself, how dangerous you can be."

He walked away, quickly, while Larry stared after him, wondering if he had heard right.

The road into the valley was steep and winding, and for some time Larry had enough to do to keep his seat in the saddle. But soon, the road widened and became easier, and he realized that he had been smelling, again, the smoke from the burned station. Had the wind changed? He raised his head, slowing his horse to a walk. Almost at the same moment, Valdir, riding ahead, raised his arm in signal, and stopped, turning his head into the wind and sniffing, nostrils flared wide.

He said, tersely, "Fire."

"Another station?" one of the Darkovans asked.

62

Valdir, moving his head from side to side – almost, Larry thought, as if he expected to hear the sound of flames – suddenly froze, statue-still. At the same moment Larry heard the sound of a bell: a deep-toned, full-throated bell tone, ringing through the valley. It tolled over and over, ringing out in a curious pattern of sound. While the little party of riders remained motionless, still listening intently, another bell farther away, fainter, but repeating the same slow rhythm, took up the ringing, and a few minutes later, still farther away, a third bell added a deep note to the choir.

Valdir said, harshly, "It's the fire-bell! Kennard, your ears are better than mine – which ring is it?"

Kennard listened intently, stiffening in his saddle. He tapped out the rhythm with his fingers, briefly. "That's the ring from Aderis."

"Come on, then," Valdir rapped out. In another minute they were all racing down the slope; Larry, startled, jerked his reins and rode after them, as fast as he could. Keeping his seat with an effort, not wanting to be left behind, he wondered what it was all about.

As they came over the brow of a little hill, he could hear the still-clamoring bell, louder and more insistent, and see, lying in the valley below them, a little cluster of roofs – the village of Aderis. The streets were filled with men, women and children; as they rode down from the slope into the streets of the village, they were surrounded by a crowd of men who fell silent as they saw Valdir Alton.

Valdir slid from his saddle, beckoned his party closer, Larry drawing close with them. He found himself beside Kennard. "What is it, what's going on?"

"Forest fire," Kennard said, motioning him to silence, listening to the man who was still pointing toward the hills across the valley. Larry, raising his head to look where the man pointed, could see only a thick darkening haze that might have been a cloud – or smoke.

The crowd in the village street was thickening, and through it all the bell tolled on.

Kennard, turning to Larry, explained quickly, "When fire breaks out in these hills, they ring the bells from the village that sees it first, and every village within hearing takes it up.

63

Before tonight, every able-bodied man in the countryside will be here. That's the law. It's almost the only law we have that runs past the boundaries of a man's own estate."

Larry could see why; even in a countryside that scorned impersonal laws, men must band together to fight the one great impersonal enemy of fire. Valdir turned his head, saw the two boys standing by their horses, and came swiftly towards them. He looked harried and remote again, and Larry realized why some men were afraid of the Alton lord when he looked like this.

"Vardi will take the horses, Kennard. They're going to send us forward into the south slopes; they need fire-lines there. Larry – " he frowned slightly, shaking his head. Finally he said, "I am responsible for your safety. The fire may sweep down this slope, so the woman and children are being sent to the next town. Go with them; I will give you a message to someone there who can have you as a guest until the emergency is over."

Kennard looked startled, and Larry could almost read his thoughts; the look in Kennard's eyes was too much for him. Should he, the stranger, be sent to safety with the women, the infirm, the little children?

"Lord Alton, I don't – "

"I haven't time to argue," the Darkovan snapped, and his eyes were formidable. "You'll be safe enough there."

Larry felt a sudden, sharp-flaring rage, like a physical thing. *Damn it, I won't be sent out of the way with the women! What do they think I am?* Valdir Alton had begun to turn away; he stopped short, so abruptly, that Larry actually wondered for a moment if he had spoken his protest aloud.

Valdir's voice was harsh. "What is it, Larry? Be quick. I have a place to fill here."

"Can't I go with the men, sir? I – " Larry fought for words, trying to put into words some of the angry thoughts that struggled in his mind.

As if echoing his thoughts, Valdir said, "If you were one of us – but your people will hold me responsible if you are harmed . . ."

Larry catching swiftly at what Valdir had told him of

64

Darkovan codes, retorted, "But you're dealing with me, not with all my people!"

Valdir smiled, bleakly. "If that's the way you want it. It's hard, rough work," he said, warningly, but Larry did not speak, and Valdir gestured. "Go with Kennard, then. He'll show you what to do."

Hurrying to join Kennard, Larry realized that he had crossed another bridge. He could be accepted by the Darkovans on their own terms, as a man – like Kennard – and not as a child to be guarded.

After a confused interval, he found himself part of a group of horsemen, Valdir in the lead, Kennard at his side, half a dozen strange Darkovans surrounding him, riding toward the low-lying haze. As they rode, the smell of smoke grew stronger, the air heavy and thick with curious smells; flecks of dust hung in the air, while bits of black soot fell on their faces and stung their eyes. His horse grew restive, backing and whinnying, as the smoke thickened. Finally they had to dismount and lead their horses forward.

As yet, the fire had been only a smolder of smoke lying against the sky, an acrid and stinging stench; but as they came between the two hills that cut off their view of the forested slopes, Larry could see a crimson glow and hear a strange dull sound in the distance. A small rabbitlike beast suddenly scudded past, almost under their horses' hooves, blindly fleeing.

Valdir pointed. He made a sharp turn past a high hedge and came out into a broad meadow whose grayish high grass was trampled and beaten down. A large number of men and boys were milling around at the center; there was a tent pitched at the edge, and after a moment of confusion Larry realized that the random groupings were orderly and businesslike. An elderly man, stooping and hobbling, came to lead their horses away; Larry gave up his reins and hurried after Kennard to the center of the field.

A boy about his own age, in a coarse sacking shirt and leather breeches, motioned to them. He nodded to Kennard in recognition, looked at Larry with a frown and asked, "Can you use an axe?"

"I'm afraid not," Larry said.

65

The Darkovan boy listened briefly to his acent, but shrugged it aside. "Take this, then," he said, and from a pile of tools handed Larry a thing like a long-toothed, sharp rake. He waved him on. Raising his eyes to the far end of the meadow, Larry could see the edge of the forest. It looked green and peaceful, but over the tops of the trees, far away, he saw the red glare of flame.

Kennard touched his arm lightly. "Come on," he said, and gave Larry a brief wry grin. "No doubt about which way we're going, that's for sure."

Larry put the rake over his shoulder and joined the group of men and boys moving toward the distant glow.

Once or twice during that long, confused afternoon, he found himself wondering, remotely, why he had gotten himself into this, but the thought was brief. He was just one of a long line of men and boys spread out, with rakes and hoes and other tools, to cut a fire-line between the distant burning fire and the village. Crude and simple as it was, it was the oldest known technique for dealing with forest-fires – create a wide space where there was nothing for it to burn. With rakes, hoes, spades and shovels, they cleared away the dry brush and pine-needles, scraped the earth bare, chopped up the dry grass and made a wide swath of open ground where nothing could burn. Men with axes felled the trees in the chosen space; smaller boys dragged the dead trees and brush away, while behind them came the crew that scraped and shoveled the ground clear. Larry quickly had an ache in his muscles and his palms stung and smarted from the handle of the rake, but he worked on, one anonymous unit in the dozens of men that kept swarming in. When one spot was cleared they were moved on to another. Younger boys brought buckets of water around; Larry drank in his turn, dropping the rake and lowering his lips to the bucket's edge. When it was too dark to see, he and Kennard were called out of the line, their places taken by a fresh crew working by torchlight, and they stumbled wearily down the slope to the camp, lined up for bowls of stew ladled out by the old men keeping the camp, and, wrapping themselves in blankets, threw themselves down to sleep on the grass, surrounded by young men and old.

Larry woke before dawn, his throat and lungs filled with

66

smoke. He sat up. The roar of the fire sounded ominous and harsh in his ears; men were still gathered at the center of the camp space. He recognized the tall form of Valdir Alton, heard the sound of excited voices. He wriggled out of his blanket and stood upright, then was aware of Kennard, rising to his feet beside him. Against the dimness, Kennard was only a blurred form. He said, "Something's happening over there. Let's go and see."

The two boys picked their way carefully through the rows of sleeping men. As they came closer to the lighted fire, the firelight shone on a tall man in a somber gray cloak, dull-red hair splotched with white, and Larry recognized the stern, ascetic face of Lorill Hastur; close at his side, in a close-wrapped cape, shivering, was a slight and fragile woman with masses of burning, fire-red hair.

Kennard whistled softly. "A *leronis*, a sorceress – and the Hastur-Lord! The fire must be worse than we thought!" He tugged at Larry's wrist. "Come on – this I want to hear!"

Quietly they crept to the outskirts of the little group. Valdir Alton had spread a blanket on the trampled grass for the woman; she sat down, staring at the glow of the distant fire as if hypnotized.

"The fire's leaped the lines on the North slope," Valdir said. "They were too close to the flames, and had to leave the area. We brought up donkey-teams to plow lines and clear away faster. But there weren't enough people working there. We had only one clairvoyant, and he couldn't see too clearly where the fire was moving."

Lorill Hastur said, in his deep voice, "We came as quickly as we could. But there's not much we can do until the sun rises." He turned to the woman. "Where are the clouds, Janine?"

Still staring fixedly at the sky, the woman said, "Too far, really. And not enough. Seven *vars* distant."

"We'll have to try it, though," Valdir said. "Otherwise it will cross the hill to the west, and burn down – Zandru's hells, it could burn all the way to the river! We can't afford to lose that much timberland."

Larry heard the words with a strange little prickle of dread. He found himself thinking, painfully, of his own world.

With tractors and earth-movers they could cut firelines

twenty feet wide in a few hours! With chemicals, they could douse the fire from the air, and have it out within the hour! Here, they didn't even have helicopters or planes to see from the air which way the fire was moving!

Kennard looked at him a little wryly, and Larry again wondered if he had spoken aloud, but the Darkovan boy said nothing. The darkness was thinning, and through the thick sooty air the sky was flushing purple with dawn.

"What are they going to do?" Larry asked.

Kennard did not answer.

The woman motioned to Lorill Hastur; he lowered himself and sat, cross-legged, on the blanket before her. Valdir Alton stood behind them, his face wiped clean of expression, intent and calm.

The woman was holding something in her hand. It was a blue jewel, glimmering, pale in the purplish dawn, and Larry thought suddenly of the blue jewel Valdir had held in his hand when he probed the mind of the dying Ranger. A curious little prickle of apprehension ran down his spine, and he shivered in the chilly, soot-laden wind.

The three forms were motionless, tense and still as carven images. Kennard gripped at Larry's arm and Larry felt the taut excitement in his friend; he wanted to ask a dozen questions, but the intentness of the three redheaded forms held him speechless. He waited.

Minutes dragged by, slowly, and the blue jewel gleamed in the woman's hand, and Larry could almost see the tension radiating between the three of them. The pale dawn brightened, and far away at the eastern horizon a dimmer crimson glow lightened the lurid red of the faraway fire. The light strengthened, grew brighter in the pale clear sky.

Then the woman sighed softly, and Larry felt it as a palpable darkening and chill. Kennard gripped his arm, pointed upward. Clouds were gathering – thickening, moving in the pale windless sky, centering, clustering from nowhere. Thick, heavy, high-piled cumulus, thin wispy fast-moving cirrus, raced from the horizon – from all the horizons! Not moving with normal wind, but coming, collecting from all corners of the compass, the clouds gathered and darkened, piling high and higher above them. The sun was blurred away, the meadow gradually darkened and Larry shivered in the sudden chill – but not with cold. He let out his breath in a long sigh.

Kennard loosed his clenched fists. He was staring at the sky. "Clouds enough," he muttered, "if only they would rain! But with no wind, if the clouds just *sit* there – "

Larry took the murmured words as license to break his silence. Questions tumbled one over another, condensed themselves to a blurted, "How did they do that? *Did* they bring those clouds?"

Kennard nodded, not taking it very seriously. "Of course. Nothing much to that – I can even do it myself, a little. On a good day for it. And they're Comyn – the most powerful psi powers on Darkover."

Larry felt the chill run up and down his spine with cold feet. Telepathy – and now clouds moved by the power of trained minds!

His Terran training said, *Impossible, superstitious rubbish! They observed which way the clouds were moving and bolstered up their reputation by predicting that clouds would pile up for rain.* But even as he said it, he knew it was not true. He was not in the safe predictable world of Terran science now, but in the cold and alien strangeness of a world where these powers were more common than a camera.

"What now?" he asked, and as if in answer, Valdir said from the center of the circle, "Now, we pray for rain. Much good may it do us."

Then, raising his head, he saw the boys, and beckoned to them.

"Have some breakfast," he said. "As soon as it's a little lighter they'll send you out on the fire-lines again. Unless it rains."

"Evanda grant it," said the woman huskily.

Lorill Hasture raised his still face and gave Kennard a smile of greeting, which turned impassive as he saw Larry. Larry, under the man's gaze, was suddenly aware of his soot-stained face, his raw and blistered hands, the torn and sweaty state of his clothes. Then he realized that Valdir Alton was in little better state. He had vaguely noticed, yesterday, that the men on the fire-lines were of all sorts: some soft-handed, in the rich clothing of aristocrats, some in the rags of the poorest. Evidently rank made no difference; rich and poor alike worked against this common danger. Of all those in the field, only the two telepaths were unstained by hard work.

Then he saw the gray look of fatigue in the eyes of the woman, the deep lines in the face of the Hastur. *Maybe their work has been the hardest of all –*

Kennard nudged him, and he accepted, from one of the old men, a lump of bread and a battered cup of a bitter-chocolaty drink. They found an unmuddied stretch of grass and sat to eat, their ears tuned to the distant roaring of the fire.

Kennard said, grimly, "They can bring the clouds and pile them up, but they can't make them rain. Although sometimes just the sheer weight of the clouds will condense them into rain. Let's hope."

"If you had airplanes – " Larry said.

"What for?"

"On Terra, they can make rain," Larry said slowly, thinking back to half-learned lessons of his schooldays. "They seed the clouds with some chemical – crystals – silver iodide," he used the Terran word, not knowing the Darkovan one, "or even dry ice will do. I'm not sure how it works, but it condenses the clouds into rain – "

"How can ice be dry?" Kennard demanded, almost rudely. "It sounds like nonsense. Like saying dry water or a live dead man."

"It's not real ice," Larry corrected himself. "It's a gas – a frozen gas, that is. It's carbon dioxide – the gas you breathe out. It crystallizes into something like snow, only it's much, much colder than ice or snow – and it burns if you touch it."

"You're not joking?"

"I hope not," said Valdir abruptly from behind them. "Kennard, what was Larry saying to you just now? I picked it up, but I can't read him – "

With a curious prickly sensation again, Larry realized that Valdir had been well out of earshot. The Darkovan lord was looking down at him with an almost fierce intensity. He said, "Make rain? It sounds, then, as if the Terrans have a magic greater than ours. Tell me about this rainmaking, Larry."

Larry repeated what he had said to Kennard, and the older

70

man stood scowling, deep in thought. Without a word, Lorill Hastur and the frail, flame-haired woman had approached them, and stood listening.

Lorill Hastur said, "What about it, Valdir? You know something of atomic structure. Is it practical at all?"

The men who had slept in the meadow were collecting their tools now, forming in groups, getting their orders for the day's work. Larry looked at the forest edge. How green it looked. Yet about it rose the blanket of smoke and the omnipresent dull roar of the fire. Valdir turned, too, and looked at the cloud that hung over the burning woods.

He said, "Fire throws off the same gas as breath. There must be an enormous quantity of carbon dioxide going off into the air."

"We can move it into the cold of the outer sky," Lorill Hastur said. "That's easy enough. And from there, if it falls on the clouds – "

"There's no time to waste," the woman said. Her eyes were closed, her voice remote, as she added, "A fire-storm has broken out on the far side of the forest, and the main blaze is racing toward the villages there. The fire-lines will never contain it. Rain is the only hope. There is enough moisture in those clouds to kill the fire – if we could only get it out of them."

"We can try," Valdir said. The three of them went into one of those intent silences again, the very air between their still forms seeming to tremble with invisible force.

Larry looked at Kennard. "Do you know what they're going to do? How can they – ?"

"They can teleport the gas above the clouds," Kennard said. "If the cold can freeze it – "

Larry was becoming a little hardened to these curious powers now. If telepathy was possible, teleportation was only a minor step –

"If they can teleport, why don't they just teleport enough water from a river, or something, to put out the fire?"

"Too much weight involved," Kennard said gravely. "Even the clouds – they didn't move the clouds themselves, just enough air to create a wind to move them here." He fell silent, his eyes on his father, and when Larry started to speak, motioned him, impatiently, to silence.

The silence in the dawnlit meadow deepened; there was no sound at all, except for the distant, indistinct sound of the fire. The clouded sky seemed to darken, grow thick and dreary. Larry watched a group of men moving away toward the fire-lines; he and Kennard should have been with them. And they stood here, waiting, watching the three telepaths –

Abruptly there was a great WHOOSH from the distant fire; Larry, whirling round, saw a tremendous uprushing billow of smoke and flame, and seemed to feel, rather than hear, the wild roaring sound. Then silence again, hushed, tense and deep.

Above his head the clouds moved, writhed, seeming to form and reform into tossing shapes and worms of moisture; they curdled, coalesced, the sky darkened and darkened as the cloud-gray deepened.

Then the sky and cloud-layer suddenly *dissolved* – that was the only way Larry could describe it, afterward – and flowed into dark, thick lines of teeming, pouring rain. The burning forest sizzled, crackled in a sort of desperation. Great thick clouds of smoke and steam and soot billowed upward, and a rushing wind flung great sparks upward. Larry was soaked through in a moment, before the rain localized itself, pouring heavily down over the forest, but leaving the meadow untouched except by the brief spit of rain. The flames, visible over the treetops, sank and died beneath the upsurge of steam and smoke. The hissing sound grew louder, roared, then dimmed and was still.

The rain stopped.

Soaked, shivering, Larry stared in blank wonder at Valdir and the two gray-clad telepaths. They had cornered the clouds; they had harnessed the very force of the rain to combat the fire!

Valdir beckoned to the boys. They walked across the damp grass, Larry still a little dazed. He had boasted of Terran science; could it match *this*?

"That's over with, at least," Valdir said, in a tone of profound relief. "Larry, I wanted to thank you; without what you told us, none of us would have known how to do that. I hardly know how to thank you."

It was more confusing then ever. These men had forces and powers undreamed of by science – and yet they were ignorant of a simple notion like cloud-seeding! Because he could not have spoken without revealing that mixture of awe, mingled with surprise at the incompleteness of the knowledge, Larry was silent. Valdir turned to Lorill Hastur and said, "Now you can see my point, perhaps! Without their knowledge – "

But before he could finish the sentence, a wild clamor of bells broke out from the village below. Valdir stiffened; the two telepaths darted looks at one another. From further away another bell and another sounded the alarm; not now in the known pattern to signal a fire, but a wild, clamorous cry of warning. The men in the camp, the men trooping back from the dead fire, dropped their tools and axes and looked up, startled. There was a rising murmur of apprehension, of dread.

Valdir swore, furiously. "We might have known – "

Kennard looked at him in astonishment. "What is it, Father?"

Valdir's mouth twisted bitterly. "A trick – the fire was obviously set to draw us away from the villages, so that the bandits could attack in peace – and find no one to meet them but women and old men and little children!"

The fire camp, until now so orderly, was suddenly a scene of milling confusion as men formed into groups, stirred around restlessly, broke away for their horses, and within a few minutes the crowded field was almost empty, men vanishing silently in all directions. Valdir watched, tight-mouthed.

"The raiders may get a surprise," he said, at last. "They'll never guess we could have conquered such a fire so quickly. Just the same" – he looked grim and angry – "I had no chance – Tell me, Larry, how would your people handle such an attack?"

"I suppose we'd all get together and fight it," Larry said, and Valdir's mouth moved in a brief, mirthless laugh.

"Right. But they won't understand that it's as urgent as a fire – " he broke off, with a violent gesture. "Zandru seize them all! Kennard, where did they take our horses?"

Fifteen minutes later they were riding away from the village, Valdir still silent and grim, Kennard and Larry not daring to break in on his anger. Larry was still struggling with the sense of wonder. The powers these Darkovans had – and the slipshod, unsystematic way they used them!

He was beginning to formulate a theory as to why Valdir had invited him to his estate. Valdir evidently had some inkling of the value of a quality which seemed alien to the Darkovan way of life, something the Terrans had. Larry hardly knew how to describe it. It was the thing Kennard had jeered at when he said, "You Terrans can't handle your personal problems by yourselves – you have to call in everyone else." Perhaps it could be called a community spirit, or the ability to work together in groups. They didn't know how to organize; even in firefighting there had been no single leader but each group had worked separately. Even now, there was no way they could get together against the common danger of the bandits. And Valdir, who could see the history of failure behind these scattered efforts, hoped to change this old pattern. But they hadn't given him a chance.

The other Darkovans who had originally been a part of the three-day hunt – how long ago that seemed! – rode several paces behind, not wanting to break in on their master's preoccupation. To Larry, Valdir's feelings seemed as clear as if he, himself had felt them. Kennard, too, riding silently at Larry's side, was mulling it over in his mind, the disparity behind the old codes and his father's attempt to change things. To Larry it seemed almost as if Kennard spoke his thoughts aloud – his father could do no wrong, and yet how had he come to these conclusions?

Once away from the site of the fire, there was no sign of clouds or of the brief rain; only the high-hanging cloud of smoke and soot over the forest told where the fire had been. Even that had vanished behind the hills by the time they paused, where the road forked at the foot of a thickly wooded slope, to breathe the horses and to eat cold food from their saddlebags.

Kennard said idly, "It's going to be good to be home."

Larry nodded. He still ached from the unaccustomed labor in the fire-lines, and his hands were raw and blistered.

"Mine too," Kennard said, displaying his hands ruefully.

"Though you'd think they were hardened enough by now. The arms-master in the city guard wouldn't have much sympathy for me. He'd say I'd shirked sword-practice too many times."

Larry reached in his saddle-bag for the small first-aid kit he had brought along. It had the emblem of the Medical HQ on it, and Kennard looked at it curiously as Larry opened it and glanced at the small bottles and tubes.

"Here. Try some of this on your blisters," he suggested diffidently, sprinkling the powder on his own. Kennard followed suit, smelling the antiseptic curiously.

"May I see it?" Kennard examined the small bottles and tubes with interested curiosity. "Your people make the damndest things!"

"Some of yours are just as strange," Larry retorted. "The idea of telepathy still seems weird to me. And teleportation!"

Kennard shrugged. "I suppose so, though of course to me it's very simple." He looked at his father; Valdir, looking somewhat less unapproachable now, turned, nodded to his son, fished in the pocket of his jerkin and tossed something to Kennard. Kennard caught the small object – it was shrouded in a small chamois bag and wrapped in silk – and from it, drew a glimmering blue jewel.

"Of course, I'm not as good at it all as my father, but still – here, take a look in this."

Gingerly, Larry touched the blue jewel. It felt faintly warm. He hesitated, remembering how Valdir had probed the mind of the dying Ranger.

"It's all right," Kennard said gently, reassuringly. "You don't think I'd hurt you, do you?"

Abashed at his own fear, Larry looked into the blue jewel. Within the depths, faint colors seemed to move and writhe; suddenly, as he looked up at Kennard, some barrier seemed to drop. The Darkovan boy seemed nearer, and easier to understand. Larry caught, in one quick flash of understanding, a sudden blaze of Kennard's thoughts, as if the essence of his friend's personality was made clear to him: Kennard's intense pride of family, his tremendous sense of responsibility for his work, the fears with which he sometimes struggled, the warmth Kennard felt for his father and his young foster-sister, even – to Larry's shy embarrassment – the warm friendliness

Kennard felt for Larry himself, and the emotion verging on awe with which he regarded Larry's travels in space and his Terran origin . . .

All this in a brief flash, as the blueness of the jewel blazed; then it faded, the barrier dropped in place again, and Kennard was smiling at him, somewhat tentatively. It occurred to Larry that Kennard now knew as much about him as he knew about Kennard. He didn't mind – but it took some getting used to!

At least, having had a sampe of it, he couldn't doubt the existence of telepathy!

Kennard shrouded the jewel again. Larry, realizing that the medical kit was still in his other hand, thrust it quickly into his pocket.

He had no way of knowing that the moment of rapport between himself and Kennard was to save both their lives . . .

VI

They had mounted again, and had ridden for an hour, when they came to a narrow canyon between two forested hills. Between the slopes and the dark trees the place lay in shadow, for the sun was declining; Valdir, riding ahead, slowed his horse to a walk and waited for the others to come up with him.

Kennard's eyes rested questioningly on his father, and Larry, riding beside him, could follow his thoughts in that way that was still so strange to him: *I don't like this place. Every clump of brushwood could have a dozen bandits behind it. It's a perfect set-up for an ambush . . . It would be my first fight. The first time I've been this close to real danger, not just lolling around the city streets chasing home troublemakers. I wonder if Father knows that I'm afraid.*

Larry's skin prickled, in a strange mixture of excitement and fear. Within the last three days his peaceful life had suddenly plunged into a maelstrom of violence and danger. It was new to him, but, somehow, not unpleasant.

They were halfway down the little valley when Larry heard, through the hoofbeats, a curious sound from deep within the bushes. He stiffened in the saddle; Valdir, alert, saw the move and reined in, looking warily around. Then, from the shelter of the trees came a harsh and raucous cry – and then mounted men were all sweeping down on them.

Valdir cried out a warning. Larry, in that first instant of petrified shock, saw the riders, tall men in long furred cloaks, long-haired and bearded, mounted on huge rangy horses of a strange breed, racing down on them at incredible speed. There was no time to flee, no time to think. Suddenly he was in the middle of the attackers, saw the Darkovans had drawn their swords; Kennard, his face very white, had his

77

dagger in his hand and was fighting to control his horse with the other.

He had a bare moment to see all this – and a strange, uprushing sense of panic that he, of all his party, was unarmed and knew nothing of fighting – before it all melted into a mad confusion of horses pushing against horses, cries in a strange tongue, the dull clash of steel on steel.

Larry's horse reared upright and plunged forward. He gripped wildly at the reins, felt them slide through his fingers, burning his blistered hands with a brief stab of pain. Then he felt himself losing his balance and slid to the ground, legs crumpling beneath him. Half stunned, he had just sense enough to roll from beneath the pawing hooves of his frantic horse. Someone tripped over his prostrate body, stumbled, fell forward on the grass; roused up with a hoarse cry of rage, and a moment later came at Larry with a knife. Larry rolled over on his back, balling up, kicking with one booted foot at the descending kife. With a split-second sense of weird unreality – *This isn't real, it can't be!* – he saw the knife spin away in a high arc and fall ten feet away. The man, knocked off balance, reeled and staggered back; recovered himself and dived at Larry, getting hold of him with both hands. Larry drew his elbows up, pushed with all his might and freed himself momentarily. He struggled up to his knees, but his attacker was on him again and the man's face – rough, bearded, with evil yellow eyes – came close and menacing. His breath stank hot in Larry's face; his hands sought for Larry's throat. Larry, frightened and yet suddenly cool-headed, found himself thinking, *He hasn't got a knife, and he's fat and out of condition.*

He went limp, relaxing and falling backward, dragging the man with him, before his attacker could recover his balance, Larry drew up his feet to his chest in an almost convulsive movement: thrust out with all his strength. The kick landed in the man's stomach. The bandit gave a yell of agony and crumpled, howling, his hands gripping his belly in obvious anguish.

Larry pulled himself up to his knees again, braced himself, and put the whole weight of his body into one punch, which struck the man fairly in the nose.

The man dropped, out cold, and lay still.

And as Larry straightened, recovering his balance, finding a moment to feel fright again, something struck him hard on the back of the head.

The clashing of swords and knives became a thunder, an explosion – then slid into a deathly, unreal silence. He felt himself falling. But he never felt himself strike the ground.

It was dark. He was sore and cramped; his whole body ached, and there was a throbbing, jolting pain in his head. He tried to move, made a hoarse sound, and opened his eyes.

He could see nothing. He knew a split-second of panic; then he began to see, dimly, through the coarse weave of cloth over his face. He tried to move his hands and felt that they were bound with cords at his side. The jolting pain went on. It felt like hoofbeats. It was hoofbeats. He was lying on his stomach, bent in the middle, and against his hands was the hairy warmth of a horse's body.

He realized, fuzzily, that he was blindfolded and flung doubled over the saddle of a horse. With the realization, he panicked and struggled to move his arms, and then felt a sharp steel point, pricking through his clothes, against his ribs.

"Lie still," said a harsh voice, in so barbarous a dialect that Larry could barely understand the words. "I know that orders are not to kill you, but you'd be none the worse for a little bloodletting – and much easier to carry! Lie still!"

Larry subsided, his head spinning. Where was he? What had happened? Where were Valdir, Kennard? Memory of the fight came rushing back. They had been outnumbered. Had the others, too, been taken prisoner? How long had he been unconscious? Where were they taking him? Cold fear gripped the boy; he was in the hands of Darkovan bandits, and he was alone and far from his own people, on a strange world whose people were hostile to Terra.

What would they do to him?

The jolting hoofbeats went on for what seemed hours before they slowed, stopped, and Larry was pulled roughly to the ground.

"A good prize," said a voice, speaking the same harsh and barbarous dialect, "and earnest for good behaviour from those sons of Zandru. The heir to Alton, no less – see the colors he wears?"

"I thought Alton's son was older than this," said another voice.

"He's small for his years," said the first voice, contemptuously, "but he bears the mark of the Comyn – hair of flame, and no commoner ever wore such clothes, or rode one of the Alton-bred horses."

"Except when we come back from a raid," guffawed another voice.

Larry went cold with fright. Was Kennard a prisoner too?

Rough hands pulled Larry forward again; the folds of muffling cloth were jerked away from his face, and someone pushed him forward. It was twilight, and it was raining a little, thin fine cold drops that made him shiver. He blinked, wishing he could get his bound hands to his head, and looked around.

They stood in the shadow of an ancient, ruined building, sharp-edged stones rising high around them. An icy wind was blowing. Larry's captor shoved him forward.

There were a good dozen of the roughnecks in the lee of the ruin, but he saw no sign of Kennard, Valdir, or of any of his companions.

Before him stood a tall, strong man, cloaked in a solid crimson mantle, much cut and torn. Under it was a dark leather vest and breeches which had once been finely cut and embroidered. The hood of the mantle was pushed back but the man's face was invisible; a soft leather mask, cut to lie close to nose and cheeks, concealed all his features to the thin cruel lips. He had six fingers on each hand. His voice was rough and husky, but he spoke the city dialect without the barbarous accent of the others.

"You are Kennard Alton-Comyn, son of Valdir?"

Larry looked around, in dismay, but no one else was visible, and suddenly his mind flashed across the mistake they had made.

They thought *he* was Kennard Alton – they had taken him as a hostage – and he dared not even tell them they had made a mistake! What would they do to one of the alien Terrans?

The man's words returned to him – *An earnest of good*

behaviour . . . the heir to Alton! That sounded as if they didn't want to kill him – not right away, at least. But how could he keep them from discovering his Terran identity? What would Kennard do?

The masked man repeated his question, harshly. Larry let out his breath, slowly and tensely. What would Kennard do – or say?

He thought of Kennard's arrogance, facing the street roughnecks a few weeks ago. He drew himself to his full height and said, clearly, slowly because he was searching for the right words and colloquial phrases, but it gave an effect of dignity, "Is it not courtesy in your land to declare the host's name before asking the name of a – a guest?"

He knew he was playing for his life. He had watched the arrogance of the Darkovan aristocrats, and he sensed that their contempt for these bandits was as great as their hatred for them. He shrugged his cloak around his shoulders – thank God he had been wearing Darkovan clothes! – and stood unflinching before the man's masked stare.

"As you wish," the masked man said, his lips curling, "yet build no hope on courtesy, son of the *Hali-imyn*. I am called Cyrillon of the Forest Roads – and you are Kennard N'Caldir Alton-Comyn."

Larry said, "Would it profit anything to deny it?"

"Very little." Behind the mask, Larry felt Cyrillon's eyes sharp on him.

"What do you want with me?"

"Not your death, unless" – the cruel lips hardened – "you make it necessary. A pawn you are, son of Alton, and of value to us, but a time could come – never doubt it – where your death would be wiser than your life in our hands. So don't build too heavily on your safety, *chiyu*, or think that you can make whatever move you please and that we won't dare to kill you for it."

He regarded Larry for a long moment, with eyes so grim that Larry flinched. He was cold with terror; he felt like breaking down, shrieking out the mistake they were making.

At last Cyrillon released his eyes. "We have a long way to ride, in rough country. You will come with us, or be carried like a bundle of blankets. But on the roads we will travel.

Men need their limbs, their wits, and the use of their eyes. The passes are not easy even for free men. If I leave you free, and give you the use of all three, will you pledge me your honor as *comyn* to make no attempt to escape?"

It occurred to Larry that a promise made under threat was no honorable promise, and involved nothing. He would, doubtless, save himself a lot of trouble by giving his parole. He wavered a moment; then, clearly as sight, he seemed to see the face of Kennard – stern, with boyish pride and the severe Darkovan concept of honor. Could a Terran do anything less? That pride stiffened his voice as he resolved to play his part.

"A pledge of honor to a thief and an outlaw? A man who" – again his thoughts raced, remembering stories Valdir had told about the codes of battle – "a man who carries away his enemy's son muffled in a cloak, rather than cutting him down openly in fair fight?"

He hesitated, then the words came to him, almost as if he heard Valdir's self speak them. "You who break laws of the road and the laws of war have no right to exchange words of honor with honorable men. I will speak to you as an equal only with the sword. Since you are without honor, I will not soil even my bare word. If you want me to go anywhere, you will have to take me by force, because I will not willingly go one step in the company of renegades and outlaws!"

Breathless, he fell silent. Cyrillon regarded him in deadly silence, his lips set and menacing, for so long that Larry quailed, and it was all he could do to keep his face impassive. Why had he burst out like that? What nonsensical impulse to play the part of an Alton had impelled those words? They had rushed out without his conscious control; without even a second thought! It might have been wiser not to enrage the outlaw.

And enrage him he had; Cyrillon's odd hands were clenched on his knife-hilt till the knuckles stood out, white and round, but he spoke quietly.

"Fine words, my boy. See, then, that you do not whimper at their results. Tie him, Kyro, and make a good job of it this time," he said to someone behind Larry.

The man cut the cords on Larry's wrists, then pulled his hands forward. He tied them together with a thick wool scarf which he took from his own throat; then the wool padding was crossed with tight leather thongs which, without the padding, would have bitten deep into his flesh. They left his feet free, but passed a rope about his waist, securing it by a long loop to the saddle of his captor. Then the man took water and wet the leather knots. Cyrillon watched these proceedings grimly and, at last, said, "I speak these orders in your presence, Alton, so that you will know what to expect. I do not want you killed; you are more useful to me alive. Just the same, Kyro, if he tries to run from the path, cut the sinew in one of his legs. If he tries to drag and hamper our climbing, once we get on the mountain, cut his throat right away. And if he makes any disturbance whatsoever as we go along the Devil's Shelf, cut the rope and let him drop down into the abyss, and good riddance to him."

Larry felt his heart suck and turn over; but although his cheeks blanched, his eyes did not falter, and, at last, Cyrillon said, "Good. We understand one another." He turned to mount, and Larry, somehow, sensed that he was disappointed.

He wanted me to be frightened and plead with him. He would get some kind of satisfaction out of seeing an Alton pleading – with him! How did I know that?

The man who had him captive lifted Larry to the back of his horse.

"For the moment we can ride," he said, grimly. He looked ill-pleased. "Don't give me any trouble, lad; I have no stomach for torturing even a whelp of the *Hali-imyn*. Never doubt he means what he says, either."

The other bandits were mounting. Larry, stiff and cold and frightened, looked up at the high wall of mountains that rose ahead.

And yet, for all his fear, a curious and unquenchable pulse of excitement and curiosity beat within him. He had wanted to see the strange and exciting life of the alien world – and here at the foot of the strange mountains, under a strange sun, he was seeing it undiluted. Even with Kennard, there had been the sense that somehow everything was a little different, because he was Terran, because he was alien.

He realized that he had really no grounds for even the

83

slight optimism he felt. For all he knew, Valdir and Kennard, and all their companions, might be lying dead in the valley where they had been ambushed. He was being taken – alone, unarmed, a prisoner, an alien – into some of the wildest and most dangerous and impassable country on Darkover.

Yet the indefinite lift of optimism remained. He was alive and unhurt – and almost anything could happen next.

VII

Larry was dreaming.

In his dream he was back on Earth, and Darkover was still a faraway, romantic dream. He was on a camping trip, sleeping out in an old forest (or why would he be so cold, with the cold dampness of rain in all his bones?).

Then, through the dream, there was a faint blue glimmer, and an urgent voice speaking. *Where are you? Where are you? We've been close enough for a long enough time, that if I can pick you up I can follow you and find you. But don't let them know you're Terran . . .*

Half impatiently he tried to shut the urgent voice away, to recapture the peaceful dream. He was back in the Terran Zone; in a little while his father would come in and waken him . . . Someone had left the air-conditioning turned up to maximum; it was cold in here, colder than even the Darkovan night . . . and what was the matter with his arm? Why was his bed so cold, had he fallen asleep on the floor? With a little groan, he rolled over, his eyes blinked open and he was back in the terrible present. He squeezed his eyes shut again, with a spasm of despair. He was in the mountain fort of the bandits, and he was very helplessly a captive and alone, and although during the day he could keep up some hope, just now he was only a frightened boy, frightened in a strange world.

His left arm had been cruelly forced backward and strapped behind his back, the left hand at the shoulder-blade, in a sort of leather harness. The fingers had long ago gone numb. The first night of his capture, the man who had carried him along the mountain trail had lifted him – numb and helpless – from the saddle, and brought him to their fire; he had, half pityingly, thrown a blanket across him, and cut the thongs on his wrist so that he could eat. Then the masked man had

85

given orders, and two of the men had brought the leather harness. They had begin to tie his right hand behind his back when Cyrillon, whose cold eyes seemed to be everywhere at once, said harshly, "Are you blind? The little *bre'suin* is left-handed."

They had not been gentle, but he had not tried to fight or struggle; the fear was still on him, but he would not give them the satisfaction of pleading. Only once, in despair, had he thought of the last resort – telling them he was not their coveted hostage –

But then what? They probably wouldn't even bother with a prisoner of no importance; they might even kill him out of hand. And he did not want to die; although now, cold, wretched and in pain, he thought it might be rather nice to be dead.

He turned over, painfully, and looked about his prison.

A grim, pale light was sneaking its way through windows curtained roughly with threadbare tapestry, and shuttered with nailed boards. The room was spacious, with worm-eaten paneling, the hangings musty with age. The bed on which he lay was large and elaborate, but there were neither bed-coverings nor sheets; only an old horsehair mattress and a couple of fur rugs. The other furniture in the chamber was rickety and depressing, but he supposed he was lucky that he wasn't in a dirty dungeon somewhere; his brief glimpse of the outside of the fort looked as if there were dungeons aplenty beneath the grim stone walls.

He had not, so far, been harmed. He had, such as it was, the freedom of this room. He could feed himself after a fashion with his right hand, but he had never realized how helpless anyone was with only one arm; he could not even balance properly when he walked. Morning and night they brought him food; a sort of coarse bread stuffed with nuts, a rough porridge of some unknown cereal, strips of rather good meat, some anonymous soapy-tasting stuff that he supposed was a form of cheese.

Now he sat up, hearing steps in the hall. It might have been someone with his breakfast, but he recognized the heavy, uneven tread of Cyrillon des Trailles. Cyrillon had visited him only once before, to inspect, briefly, the contents of his pockets.

"No weapons," the man Kyro had told him, holding up the things Larry had carried. Cyrillon turned them over. At the Terran medical kit he frowned curiously, then tossed it into a corner; Larry's mechanical pencil he tested with a fingertip, thrust into his own pocket. The other items he looked at briefly and dumped beside the Terran boy; a few small coins, a crumpled handkerchief, a small notebook. Larry's folded pocketknife he looked at curiously, asked, "What's this?"

Larry opened it, then mentally kicked himself; he might have been able to use the knife somehow, even though the main blade was broken off – he used it mostly for cutting string or building models. It had a corkscrew, a magnetized smaller blade and a hook for opening food cartons, too.

Kyro said, "A knife? You won't want to leave him that!"

Cyrillon shrugged contemptuously. "With a blade not as long as my little finger? Much good may it do him!" He dropped it with the other oddments. "I only wanted to know if he had any of the Comyn weapons." He had laughed loudly, and walked out of the room, and Larry had not seen him again until, this morning, he heard his heavy tread.

He felt a childish impulse to crawl under the bed and hide; but he mastered it, and got shakily to his feet. Three men entered, followed in a moment by Cyrillon, still masked.

Larry had realized, by now, that for all his contempt, Cyrillon treated him with a respect that verged on wariness. Larry couldn't quite figure out why. Cyrillon stood back from the bed, now, as he ordered, "Get up and come with us, Alton."

Larry rose meekly and obeyed. He had sense enough to know that any gesture of defiance wouldn't help anything – except his pride – and might bring more abusive treatment. He might as well save his strength until he could do something really effective.

They conducted him to a room where there was a fire, and Larry's shivering became so intense that Cyrillon, with a gesture of contempt, motioned him to the fireplace. "These Comyn brats are all soft . . . warm yourself, then."

87

When he was warmed through, Cyrillon gestured him to sit on bench. From a leather pouch Cyrillon drew something wrapped in a cloth. He glanced at Larry, curling his lip.

"I hardly dare to hope you will make this easy for me – or for yourself, young Alton."

He took from the cloth a jewel stone that flashed blue – a stone, Larry realized abruptly, of the same strange kind Kennard had shown him. This one was set into a ring of gold, with two handles on either side.

"I require you to look into this for me," Cyrillon said, "and if you find it easier to your pride, you may tell your people, afterward, that you did so under the threat of having your throat cut."

He laughed, that horrible raucous laughter that was like the screaming of some bird of prey.

Did Cyrillon expect him to demonstrate some psi power? Larry felt a pang of fright. His impersonation of a Darkovan must certainly fail, now. He felt his hand tremble as Cyrillon put the stone into it. He raised his eyes . . .

Blinding pain thrust through his head and eyes; he squeezed them shut spasmodically against the unbearable sense of *twisting* . . . of looking at something that should not exist in normal space at all. He felt sick. When he opened his eyes, Cryillon was looking at him in grim satisfaction.

"So. You have the sight but are not used to stones of such power. Look again."

Larry, eyes averted, shook his head in refusal.

Cyrillon rose; every movement instinct with menace. Quite calmly, without raising his voice, he said, "Oh, yes you will." He gripped Larry's bound arm, somehow exerting a pressure that made red-hot wires run through the injured shoulder. "Won't you?"

Half senseless, Larry slumped forward on the bench. The stone rolled from his lax hand and he felt himself sinking beneath a warm, dark and somehow pleasant unconsciousness.

"Very well," said Cyrillon, very far away, "give him some *kirian*."

"Too dangerous," protested one of the men. "If he has the power of some of the Altons . . ."

88

Cyrillon said impatiently, "Didn't you see him turn sick at the sight of the stone? He hasn't any power yet! We'll chance it."

Larry felt one of the men seize his head, force it backward: the other was, with great care, uncapping a small vial from which rose strange colorless fumes. Larry, remembering Valdir's probing of the dying Ranger – what had he done? – jerked his head back, struggling madly; but the man who held him pressed his thumbs on Larry's jaw, forcing it open, and the other emptied the vial into his mouth.

He struggled, expecting heat, acid fumes, but to his surprise the liquid, though bitterly cold, was almost tasteless. Almost before it touched his tongue, it seemed to evaporate. The sensation was intensely unpleasant, as if some strange gas were exploding in his head; his sight blurred, steadied. Cyrillon held the stone before his eyes; he realized, to his sick relief, that it was now only a blue glare, with none of the sickening twisting.

Cyrillon watched, intently.

Like shadows moving in the blue glare, forms became clear to Larry. A group of men rode past, Valdir's tall form clearly recognizable, a pair of curiously configured hills behind them. This faded, blurred into the face of Lorill Hastur, shrouded in a gray hood, and behind it Larry dreamily recognized the outline of the spaceport HQ building. He saw blurs again, then a small sturdy figure on a gray horse, bent low and racing against the wind, gradually cleared before his eyes . . .

Larry suddenly became aware of what was happening. Somehow, through this magical stone, he was seeing pictures and they were being transmitted to Cyrillon des Trailes – why, why? Was he trying to spy through Larry on the people of the valleys? With a cry, Larry threw his arm over his eyes and saw the pictures thin out, blur and dissolve. A blind fury surged up in him at the cruel man who was using him this way – using, he thought, Kennard Alton against his own people – and such a flare of hatred as he had never felt for a living being. He would like to blast him down . . .

And as the wrath surged up high and red, Cyrillon des Trailles drew a gasping breath of agony, dashed the crystal out of his hand and, with agonized force, struck Larry across the face. Larry fell, heavily, to the floor, and Cyrillon, doubled over in anguish, aimed a kick at him, missed and sank wearily to the bench.

One of the men said, "I warned you not to give him *kirian*. You gave him too much."

Cyrillon said, his voice still thick, "I guessed better than I knew . . . the accursed race have whelped a throwback! The youngster didn't even know what he was doing! If I had one or two of that kind in my hands, the whole cursed race of Cassild' would flee back to their lake-bottoms, and the Golden-Chained one would reign again! Zandru, what we could do with one of them on our side!"

The other man said, "We ought to kill him out of hand, before they find some way to use him against us!"

"Not yet," said Cyrillon. "I wonder how old he is? He looks a child, but all those lowland brats are soft."

One of the men guffawed. "He seemed not so soft a moment ago, when he had you yelping like a scalded cat!"

Cyrillon said, very softly, "If he were really as young as he looks, I'd guarantee to re-educate him in my own way. I may try, at any rate. I can bear more than that," he added with gentle menace, "until he learns to – control his powers."

Larry, lying on the floor very still and hoping they had forgotten him, struggled with puzzlement greater than fear. Had *he* done that? If so, how? *He* had none of these Darkovan powers!

One of the men bent. Not gently, he lifted Larry to his feet. Cyrillon said, "Well, Kennard Alton, I warn you fairly not to try that trick again. Perhaps it was sheer reflex and you do not know your own powers. If that is true, I warn you, you had better learn control. The next time I will kick your ribs through your backbone. Now – *look into the stone!*"

The blue glare blinded his eyes. Then, crystal bright, intense, there were figures and forms he could not interpret, coming and going . . . How was Cyrillon doing this? Or was he simply being hypnotized?

The blueness suddenly flared again. Inside his mind, in a sudden blaze, the voice of his dream spoke, *I've blanked it. He's no telepath and he doesn't dare force you. Don't be afraid;*

90

*he can't read what you're getting now – but I can't hold this for
long . . . It's not hopeless yet . . .*

Kennard?

Larry thought, *I'm going out of my mind . . .*

The blue glare spread, became unbearable. He heard
Cyrillon snarl something – a threat? – but he saw nothing
but that fearful blue.

With utter, absolute relief, for the first time in his life, Larry
Montray fainted.

VIII

Day followed slow day, in the room where Larry was imprisoned; gradually, his original optimism dimmed out and faded. He was here, and there was no way to tell whether or not he would ever leave the place. He now knew he was being held as a hostage against Valdir Alton. From scraps of information he had wormed out of his jailer, he had put together the situation. Cyrillon and others of his kind had preyed on the lower lands since time out of mind. Valdir had been the first to organize the lowlanders in resistance, to build the Ranger stations which warned of impending raids, and this struck Cyrillon, unreasonably enough, as unfair. It ran clear against the time-honored Darkovan code, that each man shall defend his own belongings. By holding Valdir's son prisoner, he hoped to stalemate this move, and ward off retaliations.

But they did *not* have Valdir's son; and sooner or later, Larry supposed, Cyrillon would find it out. He didn't like to think what would happen then.

As the fourth day was darkening into night, he heard sounds in the distance; feet hurrying in the corridors, horses' hooves trampling in the courtyard, men calling to one another in command. He looked up, in frustration, at the high window which prevented him from seeing out; then dragged a heavy bench toward the window and clambered up on it. He could just see over the broad, high sill, and down into the courtyard below.

Nearly two dozen men were milling around below, leading out and saddling horses, choosing weapons from a great pile in the corner of the bricked-in courtyard. Larry saw Cyrillon's form, tall and lean, striding through the men; here pausing to speak to one, here inspecting a saddle-girth, here lashing out, swift as a striking snake, to knock a man head-over-heels with a swift fist. The great gate was swinging open, the mounted men forming to ride through.

92

Was the castle empty, then? Unguarded? Larry looked down to the courtyard, in frustration. He was at least thirty feet above the bricks; a thirty-foot fall might not kill him if he landed on grass, but on stone . . . ? The castle wall was smooth below him for at least ten feet; with the use of both hands, he might well have managed a foothold on the ledge below. With one hand tied behind his back, he might as well have tried to walk a tightrope to the nearest mountain peak.

He let himself slide down to the floor again. Doubtless they had left someone here . . . possibly only the feeble old man who brought Larry's food.

If he had a weapon . . .

They had left him his pocketknife; but the main blade was broken, and the magnetized blade remaining was less than two inches long. The furniture in the room was all old and too heavy to be broken up for a club of any sort. If he could somehow manage to club the man over the head when next he came in . . .

There seemed nothing from which he could improvise even a simple weapon. With both hands, he might have thrown his jacket at the old man and managed to smother him with it. They seemed to be guarding against the Comyn telepathic tricks, but they had not tried to guard against ordinary attack . . . and yet there was nothing in the room that could be used as a weapon.

He sat, scowling, considering, for a long time. If he could have smashed the window, perhaps a long splinter of glass might serve.

He heard shuffling footsteps down the hall, and a thought – almost too late! – occurred to him. He dropped to the floor and, with his one free hand, fumbled to unlace his boot. It was heavy, a Darkovan riding-boot, and if it struck the man on the back of the head –

But it was slow work with one hand and before he had it off, a key moved in the lock, the door came open in one burst, as if the man had stood back and kicked it open without coming inside. Then the man appeared in the door. He had a tray with food balanced in one hand; the other held a long, wicked-looking riding whip. He held it poised to strike, saying in his barbarous dialect, "None of your tricks, boy!"

93

Larry jerked off the boot, clumsily with his right hand, and hurled it at the man's head.

As soon as he had thrown it, he knew that the throw, with the wrong hand, would go wild; he saw the old man start slightly, the dishes on the tray clashing together. The whip, as if with a life of its own, flicked out and wrapped round Larry's free wrist, with a stinging slap; the man jerked the whip free, laughing harshly.

"I thought you might have some such little trick," he jerked, raised the whip again and brought it down, not very hard, across Larry's shoulders. Tears started to Larry's eyes, but really it was more of a warning than a blow – for Larry knew that a blow with such a whip, given seriously, would cut through his clothes and an inch into the flesh.

"Want some more?" the man asked, with a grin.

Furious with frustration, Larry bent his eyes on the ground.

The man said good-naturedly, "Eat your dinner, lad. You don't try any tricks and I won't hurt you – agreed? No reason we can't get along very nicely while the Master is away – is there?"

When the man had gone, Larry turned dispiritedly to the tray. He didn't feel like eating; yet he had eaten so little in the last four days that he was tormented with hunger. The final ignominy was that he couldn't even get his boot on with one hand. He took the dishes off the tray, listlessly. Then he raised his eyebrows; instead of the usual dried meat strips and coarse bread, there was some sort of grilled fish, smoking hot, and a cup of the same chocolate-like drink he had had in the Trade City.

Awkwardly, with his free hand, but hungrily, he gobbled down the fish, even gnawing on the bones. It was an unfamiliar fish and had a strange tang, but he was too hungry to be particular. He leaned back, sipping the drink slowly. He wondered about the change. Perhaps Cyrillon – who obviously was somewhat afraid of him since the episode with the crystal – considered him valuable as a hostage and, seeing the coarser food left uneaten, had decided he had to feed him better, and keep him in good health and good spirits.

The light from the high window crept across the floor. The shadows were pale purple, the light pink and sparkling. Strange motes danced in the pink beam.

Larry, feeling full and comfortably sleepy, leaned back, watching the motes. He realized suddenly that on each of the motes a tiny man rode, pink and purple and carrying an infinitesimal spear that looked like a fiber of saffron. Fascinated, incurious, he watched the tiny men slide down the sunbeam and mass on the floor. They formed into regiments, and still they kept sliding down the beam of pink light, until their small forms covered the floor. Larry blinked and they seemed to merge and melt away.

A huge black insect, almost the width of Larry's hand, stuck his quivering head from a hole in the floor. He waggled huge phosphorescent whiskers at Larry and spoke . . . and to Larry's listless interest, the bug was speaking perfect Terran.

"You're drugged, you know," the bug said in a high, shaky voice. "It must have been in the food. Of course, that's why it was so much better than usual this time, so you'd be sure to eat it."

The pink and purple men reappeared on the floor and swarmed over the bug, shrilling in incomprehensible voices, nonsense syllables: "*An chrya morgobush! Travertina fo mibbsy!*"

As each little man touched the bug's phosphorescent tendrils, he burst into a puff of green smoke.

The door swung open, invitingly. Someone said in the distance, "No tricks this time, hah?"

The man was standing there, and the twilight in the room darkened, brightened again into dawn. The man with the whip jeered from a corner. The little pink and purple men were crawling all over him and Larry laughed aloud to see his jailer covered with the swarming creatures; one of them disappeared into his pocket, another did a hornpipe on the man's bald head. Dimly he felt someone bend over him, shove up his closed eyelid. How could he see with closed eyes? He laughed at the absurdity of it.

"No tricks," said the jailer again; and all the little pink and purple men shouted in chorus, "'No tricks,' he said!"

Behind the man the door opened and Kennard Alton, in dark-green cloak and a drawn dagger in his hand, stood there. The little pink and purple men swarmed up his legs and nearly blotted out his figure. He raised the dagger and it turned into a bunch of pink tulips as he brought it down toward the old bandit's back. Larry heard himself laugh, but the laugh came out like a tumpetblast as the pink tulips plunged into the man's back and a great flight of blackbirds gushed out, screaming wildly. Kennard kicked the fallen man, who disappeared into a swarming regiment of little pink and purple men laughing in isolated notes like small bells. Then Kennard strode across the room. The purple men swarmed up him, sat astride his nose, soared down the sunbeams, as Kennard stood over Larry.

"Come on! Every minute we're here, there's danger! Somebody might come. I'm not sure that old fellow's the only guard in the castle!"

Larry looked up at him and laughed idly. The little pink and purple mannikin on Kennard's nose was climbing up, digging footholds in Kennard's chin with a tiny ax of green light. Larry laughed again.

"Brush the gremlins off your chin first."

"Zandru!" Kennard bent over, pink tulips cascading from the front of his shirt. His hands clasped on Larry's shoulders like nutcrackers. "I want some nuts," Larry said, and giggled.

"Damn you, get up and come with me."

Larry blinked. He said clearly, in Terran, "You're not really here, you know. Any more than the little pink and purple gremlins are here. You're a figment of my imagination. Go away, figment. A figment with purple pigment."

The figment bent over Larry. In his hands there seemed to be a bowl of chili with beans. He began throwing it at Larry, handful by handful. It was unpleasant; Larry's head hurt and the beans, dripping off his chin, hurt like hard slaps. He yelled in Darkovan, "Save the beans! They're too hard! We might better eat them!"

The vision-Kennard straightened as if he had been knifed. He muttered, "*Shallavan!* But why did they give it to Larry? *He's* no telepath! Did they believe – "

Larry protested as Kennard turned into a steamshovel and lifted him sidewise. The next thing he knew, water was streaming down his face and Kennard Alton, white as a sheet, was standing and staring at him.

It was Kennard. He was real.

Larry said shakily "I – I thought you were a – a steamshovel. Is it – "

He looked down at the floor of the room. The old man lay there, blood caked on his leather jacket, and Larry hastily turned away. "Is he dead?"

"I don't know and I don't care," Kennard said grimly, "but we'll *both* be dead unless we get out of here before the bandits get back. Where's your other boot?"

"It threw it at him." Larry's head was splitting. "I missed."

"Oh, well – " Kennard said, deprecatingly, "you aren't used to this sort of thing. Get it on again – " he broke off. "What in the devil – " He surveyed the leather harness, anger in his eyes. "Zandru's hells, with a filthy contrivance!" He drew his dagger and cut through the leather. Larry's hand, numb and cramped, fell lifeless to his side. He could not move the fingers, and Kennard, swearing under his breath, knelt to help him with the boot.

Larry realized that he had no idea how long he had been drugged. He had a vague sort of memory of his jailer having come in once or twice before, but was not sure. He was still too dazed to do more than stand, swaying and weak, before Kennard.

"How did you come to be here? How did you find me?"

"You were taken for me," Kennard said briefly. "Could I leave you to face the fate they meant for me? It was my responsibility to find you."

"But how? And why did you come alone?"

"We were in rapport through the crystal," Kennard said, "so I could trail you. I came alone, because we knew that with any assault in strength, they'd probably kill you at once. That can wait till later! Right now, we still have to get out of this place before Cyrillon and his devils come back!"

"I saw them ride away," Larry said slowly. "I think they're all gone except that one old man."

"No wonder they doped you, then," Kennard said. "They'd be afraid you'd play some telepathic trick. Most people are afraid of the Altons, though they wouldn't know if you were old enough to have the *laran* – the power. I don't have much of it myself. But let's get out of here!"

Carefully he went to the door and opened it a fraction. "The

97

way he yelled, if there was anyone within shouting distance, they'd be all over us," Kennard said. "I think maybe you're right. They all must have gone."

Carefully, they came out into the corridor; walking on tiptoe, stole down the long stairs. Once Kennard muttered, "I hope we don't meet anyone! If I don't go out the way I came in, it would be damned easy to get lost in this place!"

Larry had not realized how immense this bandit stronghold was. He came out of the prison room wavering, unsteady on his feet so that Kennard had to take hold of his arm and brace him until he could stand without shaking. Still groggy from the drug, it seemed that they hurried through miles of corridors, starting at every distant sound, flattening themselves against the walls when once something like a step echoed at the bottom of a flight of stairs. But it had died in the distance and the old castle was silent again, brooding.

A great gate loomed before them and Kennard, shoving Larry back against the wall, peered out, sniffing the wind like a hunter. He said, tersely, "Seems quiet enough. We'll chance it. It don't know where the other gates are. I saw them ride way and took the chance."

The fresh air, bitterly cold, seemed to bite at Larry's bones, but it cleared the last traces of the drug from his head, and he stood staring round. Behind them, a high steep mountain face towered, rocky, speckled faintly with a scruff of underbrush and trees. Before them the narrow trail led away downward, through the valleys and hills, through the mountains where they had come.

Kennard said, swiftly, "Come on – we'll make a dash for it. If anyone's watching from those windows – " He made an edgy gesture upward toward the black castle face behind them. "If that old fellow *isn't* dead, and there *are* other guards, we've got maybe an hour before they start beating the woods for us."

He poised, said briefly, "Now – run," and raced across the yard toward the gates, Larry following. His arm ached fiercely where it had been strapped, and he was shaky on his feet, but even so, he reached the edge of the forest only a few seconds after Kennard, and the Darkovan boy looked at him a little less impatiently. They stood there, breathing hard, looking at each other in wordless question. What next?

98

"There's only one road through these mountains," Kennard said, "and that's the one the bandits used. We could follow it – keeping in sight of it, and hiding if we heard anyone. There's an awful lot of forest between here and home – they couldn't search it all. But" – he gestured – "I think they have watch-towers too, all through this country along the road. We ought to stay under cover of the trees, night and day, if we take that route. This whole stretch of country – " he stopped, thinking hard, and Larry saw vividly, in his mind's eye, the terrible journey over chasms and crags which had brought him here. Kennard nodded.

"That's why they don't guard their stronghold, of course, they think themselves guarded well enough by the mountain trail. You need good, mountain-bred, trail-broken horses to make it at all. I left my own horse on the other side of the mountain ridge. Somebody's probably picked her up by now. I'd hoped – "

The deep throat of an alarm bell suddenly clanged, raising echoes in the forest; a bird cried out noisily and flew away, and Kennard started, swearing under his breath.

"They've roused the whole castle – there must have been some of them left there!" he said, tensely, gripping Larry's arm. "In ten minutes this whole part of the woods will be alive with them! Come on!"

He ran – feeling twigs catch and hold at his clothing, stumbling into burrows and ridges, his breath coming short in the bitter cold. Before him Kennard dodged and twisted, half doubling back once and again, plunging through the trackless trees, and Larry, stumbling and racing in desperate haste to keep up, his head pounding, fled after him.

It seemed hours before Kennard dropped into a little hollow made by the fallen branches of a tree. Larry dropped at his side, his head falling forward against the icy-wet grass. For a few moments all that he could do was to breathe. Slowly the pounding of his heart calmed to something like normal and the darkness cleared from before his eyes. He raised himself half on his elbow, but Kennard jerked him down again.

"Lie flat!"

Larry was only too glad to obey. The world was still spinning; after a moment it spun completely away.

When he came up to consciousness again, Kennard was kneeling at his side, head raised, his ear cocked for the wind.

"They may have trackers on our trail," he said, tersely. "I thought I heard – Listen!"

At first Larry's ears, not trained to woodcraft, heard nothing. Then, very far away, lifting and rising in a long eerie wail, a shrill banshee scream that grew in intensity until his ears vibrated with the sound and he clasped his hands to his head to shut out the sheer torture of the noise. It faded away; rose again in another siren wail. He looked at Kennard; the older boy was stark white.

"What is it?" Larry whispered.

"Banshees," Kennard said, and his voice was a gasp. "They can track anything that lives – and they'll scent our body warmth. If they get wind of us we're done for!" He swore, gasping, his voice dying away in a half-sob. "Damn Cyrillon – damn him and his while evil crew – Zandru whip them with scorpions in his seventh hell – Naotalba twist their feet on their ankles– " His voice rose to a half-scream of hysteria. He looked white with exhaustion. Larry gripped his shoulders and shook him hard.

"That won't help! What will?"

Kennard gasped and was silent. Slowly the color came back into his face and he listened, motionless, to the siren wail that rose and fell.

"About a mile off," he said tersely, "but they run like the wind. If we could change our smell – "

"They're probably tracking by my clothing smell," Larry said. "They took away my cloak. If I – "

Kennard had risen; he darted forward, suddenly, and fell into a bank of grayish shrubs. For a moment, Larry, watching him roll and writhe in the leaves, thought that the hardships of the mountain journey had driven the Darkovan boy out of his wits. But when Kennard sat up his face, though ashen, was calm.

"Come here and roll in this," he ordered, "smear it all over your boots especially – "

Suddenly getting the idea, Larry grabbed handfuls of the leaves. They stung his hands with their furry needles, but he followed the older boy's example, daubing the leaves on face and hands, crushing their juice into clothing and boots. The leaves had a pungent, acrid smell that brought tears to his eyes like raw onions; but he crushed handfuls of the leaves over his boots and legs.

"This might or might not work," Kennard said, "but it gives us a bare chance – unless the smell of this stuff is like catnip to a kitten for those devilish things. If I knew more about them – "

"What are they?"

"Birds. Huge things – taller than a tall man, with long trailing thin wings – they can't fly. Their claws could rip your guts out at a stroke. They're blind, and normally they live in the mountain snows, and can scent anything warm that moves. And they scream like – well, like banshees."

All the time he spoke, he and Larry were crushing the leaves, rubbing them into their skin and hair, soaking their clothing with the juice. The odor was sickening and Larry thought secretly that anything with any sense of smell at all could trace them for miles, but perhaps the banshees were like Terran bloodhounds, set on by a particular smell and trained not to follow any other.

"Zandru alone knows how Cyrillon and his hordes managed to train those devilish things," Kennard muttered. "Listen – they're coming nearer. Come on. We'll have to run for it again, but try to move quietly."

They moved off through the brushwood again, working their way slowly up the hill, Larry trying to move softly; but he heard dead twigs snap beneath his feet, dry leaves crackle, the creak of branches as he moved against them. In contrast, Kennard moved as lightly as a leaf. And ever behind them the shrill banshee howl rose, swelled, died away and rose again, throbbing until it seemed to fill all space, till Larry felt he must scream with the noise that vibrated his eardrums and went rolling around in his skull until there was no room for anything but pulsing agony.

The path they were following began to rise, steeply now, and he had to catch at twigs and brushwood, and brace his feet against rocks, to force his way up the rising slope. His clothes were tattered, his face torn, and the stink of the gray leaves was all around them. The slope was in deep shadow; it was growing bitterly cold, and above them the

101

thick evening fog was deepening, till Larry could hardly see Kennard's back, a few feet before him. They struggled up the slope and plunged down into a little valley, where Kennard's pace slackened somewhat and he waited for Larry to catch up with him. Larry breathed hard, pressing his hands to his aching skull to shut out the banshee noise.

It lessened for a moment, died away in a sort of puzzled silence; began in a series of fresh yelps and wails, then faded out again. It was dimming with distance; Kennard, his face only a blur in the gathering fog, sighed and fell, exhausted, to the ground.

"We can rest for a minute, but not too long," he warned.

Larry fell forward, dropping instantly into dead sleep. It seemed only a moment later – but it was black dark and a fine drizzling rain was falling and soaking them – that Kennard shook him awake again. The banshee howls were again filling the air – and *on this side of the slope!*

"They must have found the patch of *eris* leaves and figured out what we'd done," he said, his voice dragging between his teeth, "and, of course, that stuff leaves a scent that a broken-down mule could follow from here to Nevarsin!"

Larry strained his eyes to see through the thin darkness. Far down the slope there seemed a glint, just a pale glimmer in the moonlight. "Is there a stream at the bottom of the valley?"

"There might be. If there is – " Kennard was swaying with weariness. Larry, though aching in every muscle, found that the last traces of the drug were gone from his mind, and the brief sleep had refreshed him. He put his arm around Kennard's shoulders and guided the other boy's stumbling steps. "If we can get into the water – "

"They'll figure that trick out too," Kennard said hopelessly, and Larry felt him shudder, a deep thing that racked his bones. He pointed upward, and Larry followed his gaze. At the top of the slope, outlined against the sky, was a sight to freeze the marrow of his bones.

Bird? Surely no bird ever had that great gaunt outline, those drooping wings like a huge flapping cloak, the skull-like head that dripped a great phosphorescent red-glowing beak. The apparition craned a long dark neck and a dreadful throbbing cry vibrated to air-filling intensity.

102

Larry felt Kennard go rigid on his arm; the boy was staring upward, fixedly, like a bird hypnotized by a weaving snake.

But to Larry it was just another Darkovan horror; dreadful indeed – but he had seen so many horrors he was numb. He grabbed Kennard, and plunged with him down the slope, toward the distant glimmer. The banshee howl rose and fell, rose and fell on their heels, as they plunged through underbrush, careless now of noise or direction. The gleam of water loomed before them. They plunged in, fell full length with a splash, stuggled up and ran, splashing, racing, stumbling on stones. Twice Larry measured his length in the shallow icy stream and his clothing stiffened and froze in the icy air, but he dared not slacken his speed. The banshee howl grew, louder and louder, then slackened again in a puzzled, yelping wail, an almost plaintive series of cheated whimpers. It seemed to run round in circles. It was joined by further howls, yelps and whimpers. They splashed along in the stream for what seemed hours, and Larry's feet were like lumps of ice. Kennard was stumbling; he fell again and again to his knees and the last time he fell with his head on the bank and lay still. None of Larry's urging could make him rise. The Darkovan lad had simply reached the end of his fantastic endurance.

Larry dragged him out, on the far side of the stream, hauled him into the shelter of the forest, and sat there listening to the gradually diminishing wails and yelps of the frustrated banshees. Far away on the slope he saw torches and lights. They were beating the bushes, but with their tracking birds cheated, there was no way to follow their escaped prey. But would they pick up the scent again downstream? Larry, conscious that he was famished, remembered that a day or two ago – before the drugging – he had thrust a piece of the coarse bread into his pocket. He hauled it out and began to gnaw on it; then, remembering, broke it in half and stowed the other half in his other pocket for Kennard. As he did so, his hands touched metal, and he felt the smooth outline of his Terran medical kit. Small as it was, it probably contained nothing for his scratches and bruises, but –

Of course! He pulled urgently at Kennard's hand; when the Darkovan boy stirred and moaned, he put the bread in his hand, then whispered, "Listen, I think we can outwit them

103

even if they pick up our scent downstream. Here. Eat that, and then listen!" He was fumling in the dark, by touch, in his medical kit. He found the half-empty tube of burn ointment he had used after the fire, unscrewed the cap and smelled the sharp, unfamiliar chemical smell.

"This should puzzle them for a while," he said, smearing a thin layer of the stuff, first on his boots and then on Kennard's. Kennard, munching the bread, nodded in approval. "They might pick up *eris* leaves. Not this stuff."

They rested a little, then began cautiously to crawl up the far slope. There was plenty of cover, though the plants and thorny bushes of the underbrush tore at their faces and hands. Kennard's leather riding-breeches did not suffer so badly as Larry's cloth ones, but their hands and faces were torn and bleeding, and the red sun was beginning to thin away the dawn clouds, before they reached the summit of the slope and lay on the rocks exhausted, too weary to move another step. Behind them, in the valley they had left, there seemed no sign of men or banshees.

"They must have called off the hunt," Kennard muttered, "Banshees are torpid to the sunlight – they're nightbirds. We just might have got clean away."

Huddling his cloak round him, he knelt and looked down into the far valley. It was a huge bowl of land, filled to the brim with layered forest. Near the top, where they were, there was underbrush and low scrubby conifers, and snow lay in thin patches in hollows of the ground where the sun had not warmed. Lower down were tall trees and thick brushwood, while the valley was thick with uncleared forest. Not a house, nor a farm, not a cleared space of land, not even a moving figure. Only the wheeling of a hawk above them, and the silent trees below them, moved in response to their dragging steps. They had escaped Cyrillon's castle. But in the growing red light, their eyes met, and the same thought was in them both.

They had escaped bandits and banshees. But they were hundreds of miles from safe, known country – alone, on foot, almost weaponless, in the great trackless unexplored forests of the wildest part of Darkover.

They were alive.

And that was just about all that they could say.

IX

The sun climbed higher and higher. In the high hollow where they lay, a little cold sun penetrated their retreat, and finally Kennard stirred. He took off his cloak and spread it in the sun to dry, then stripped to the skin and gestured to Larry to do likewise. When Larry, shivering, hesitated, Kennard said harshly, "Wet clothes will freeze you faster than cold skin. And take off your boots and dry your stockings."

Larry obeyed, shivering, crouching in the lee of a sunwarmed rock. While their clothes dried in the bitter wind of the heights, they took stock.

In addition to his medical kit – which contained only a few of the most ordinary remedies, and measured only four or five inches square – Larry had his knife with the broken blade, corkscrew, and tiny magnetized blade. Kennard looked at it with raised eyebrows and a rueful grin, and shrugged. He also had another piece of the coarse bread, a notebook, handkerchief and a coin or two.

Kennard, who had come provided for a long journey, was better armed with his razor-sharp dagger, a tinderbox and flints, and in the leather pouch at his waist he had some bread and dried meat. "Not much," he said. "I had more cached near where I left my horse; I'd hoped we could dare take that road. And there is food in the forests, though I'm not so sure here as I am in the woodlands nearer home. No, we won't starve, but there's worse than that."

At Larry's questioning look, he said reluctantly, "We're lost, Larry. I lost my bearings when we were getting away from the banshees last night. All I know is that we're west of Cyrillon's hold – and no lowlander or Comyn has ever come so far into these mountains. Never. At least, if they have, they haven't lived to tell about it. We can't go back eastward toward home

– we'd have to cross Cyrillon's country – or make a wide circle northward and get into the Dry Towns." His face, though he tried to keep it impassive, trembled. "That's all desert land – sand, no water, no food, and we might as well go back and ask Cyrillon for a night's lodging. Southward there's the range of the Hellers – and not even professional guides or mountaineers will go into them without climbing equipment, and mountain gear. I've done a little rockclimbing, but I'm about as fit to climb through the Hellers as you are to navigate a Terran spaceship."

That left only one possibility. "Westward?"

"Unless we want to try to get through Cyrillon's country again, banshees and all. As far as I know, it's simply forest. It's unexplored, but if we follow the setting sun, we should come out somewhere near to the lands where Lorill Hastur has his holdings. We'll be passing to the north of the Hellers – " He drew a crude sketch-map on the ground. "We're here. And we want to get to here. But the gods alone know what's in between, or how long it will take us." He looked at Larry, steadily. "I wouldn't enjoy a trip like that, even with my father and a dozen of his huskiest soldiers. But, *bredu*, if you'll back me up, we'll try it."

He met Larry's eyes, and for an instant Larry was reminded of that moment of deep rapport between them, across the blue crystal of psychic power. The word, *bredu*, had startled him. It meant, literally, *friend* – but the ordinary word for friend was simply *com'ii. Bredu* could mean one close, as in a family relationship – cousin, or brother – or it could mean *beloved brother*. It was a word which showed him the trust that this Darkovan boy, who had saved his life, placed in him. Kennard had undertaken, alone, a desperate journey on his behalf – and was about to undertake another, with Larry's help.

It was the most solemn moment of Larry's life. He was almost paralyzed with his fear, and he could feel Kennard's fear as if it were his own; deeper, because Kennard knew more of the dangers. And yet –

Larry said quietly, "I'm ready to try it if you are – *bredu*."

And in that moment he knew that he would, if necessary, give his life for Kennard – as Kennard had risked his for him.

The moment lasted only a fraction of a second. Then

Kennard broke the remaining piece of Cyrillon's bread, and said, "Let's finish this. We need the strength. Then I have this – " Briefly, from his pocket, he showed the silk-wrapped thing that held the blue crystal. "It helped me find you, because when you looked into it, your mind was keyed to it. So that when I was lost, all I had to do was to look in it and think of you – and it showed me the right direction."

Larry averted his eyes from the stone. It made him think of that moment in Cyrillon's power. "Cyrillon made me look into one of the things."

The result on Kennard was electrifying. His whole face changed and turned white. "Cyrillon – has one of *these*?"

Briefly, Larry told him about it, and Kennard wet dry lips with his tongue. "Avarra guard and guide us! He may not know how to use it, but if he should ever learn, or if he should whelp a telepath by one of his women, the Gods themselves couldn't save Darkover from their evil powers! Not to mention," he added grimly, "that he might track us with it – as I tracked you."

"He's afraid of it," Larry said, and told Kennard how he knew, but Kennard shook his head. "He might still risk it; he'd evidently risk a lot to have you. Oh, Zandru, what shall I do, what shall I do!" He covered his face with his hands and sat motionless, the blue stone clutched in his hand. Finally he looked up and his face was gray and drawn with terror.

"We – must destroy Cyrillon's stone," he said at last. "I know what I must do, but I'm afraid, Larry, I'm afraid!" It was a cry of terror. "But I must!"

"Why?"

Kennard looked grim. He rolled back his sleeve and showed Larry a curious mark, like a tattoo. "Because I am sworn," he said, grimly, "that I will die rather than let any of our Comyn weapons fall into the hands of such people."

Larry felt a cold wrench of terror twisting his insides. To go back, deliberately, into Cyrillon's power and destroy the stone . . .

"What do we do?" he asked, deliberately light and sarcastic, "walk up to his front door and ask him politely to let us have it?"

Kennard shook his head. "Worse than that," he said, his

voice barely audible, "and I can't do it alone. I'll have to have your help. Aldones guard us! If I could only reach father with this – but I can't – "

"What is it? What do you have to do?"

"You wouldn't understand – " Kennard began hotly; then with an effort, said, "Sorry. You're in this, too, and you'll have to help me. I have to take *this*" – he motioned toward the blue crystal in his hand – and destroy Cyrillon's – with it. And we have to do it *now*."

"But how can I?" Larry was frightened and bewildered. "I am not a telepath."

"You must be," said Kennard urgently, "you fought Cyrillon to a standstill with the thing! I don't understand it either. I never heard of a Terran telepath. But evidently you and I are in rapport. Maybe you got it from me, I'm not sure. But we'll try."

He unwrapped the crystal and Larry averted his eyes. The thought of looking into the thing again made him literally sick to his stomach. The memory of Cyrillon's forcing made his abused shoulder ache in sympathy.

But Kennard had to do it – Kennard, who had risked death to save him. Larry said steadily, "What do I have to do?"

Kennard sat cross-legged, gazing into the stone, and Larry was inescapably reminded of the three Adepts who had brought the rain to the forest fire. Uncommanded, he took his place across from Kennard. Kennard said, silently, "Just go into link with me – and hold hard. Don't let go, whatever happens."

The twisting blueness of the crystal engulfed all space. Larry felt Kennard like a spot of fire and tensed, throwing all his energies, all his will toward supporting him –

He felt a blue blaze, slumbering, blaze up and waken. It flared out, flaming electric blue, and Larry felt himself struggling, drowning. His body ached, his whole head tingled, earth spun away, he reeled alone in blue space, as blue flame met blue flame and he felt Kennard tremble, spin out and vanish in unfathomable distance. The fire was drowning him . . .

Then from somewhere a huge surge of strength seemed to roar through him, the same strength that had flung Cyrillon howling across the room. He poured it against the alien blue. The flames met, merged, sank –

The forest was green and bright around them and Larry gulped in air like a drowning man. Kennard lay white and drained on the leaves, his hand limply clutching the crystal. But there was no blue fire in its heart now. It was colorless stone, which as Larry looked glimmered once or twice and evaporated in a tiny puff of blue vapor. Kennard's hand was empty.

Kennard sat up, his chest heaving. He said, "It's gone. I destroyed it – even though I had to destroy this one too. And it might have guided us to Lorill Hastur's lands." His frown was bitter. "But better than having a starstone in Cyrillon's possession. Now all we have to face are ordinary dangers. Well" – He shrugged, and struggled to his feet. "We've got a lot of country to cover, and all we have to do is to follow the sun's path westward. Let's get started."

Forcing back his multitude of question and curiosity, Larry reached out for his now-drying clothes and began to draw them on. He knew Kennard well enough, by now, to know that he had had all the explanation the other lad would ever give him. Silently, he pocketed his little knife, his medical kit, thrust his feet into his boots. Still silently, he followed Kennard as the Darkovan started down the western slope of the mountain, down into the trackless wasteland that lay between Cyrillon's castle and the lands of Lorill Hastur.

All that day and all the next they spent forcing their way down through the pathless underbrush, following the westward sun-route, sleeping at night in hollows of dead leaves, eating sparingly of the bread and meat remaining of Kennard's provision. On the night of the second day it came to an end, and they went supperless to bed, munching a few dried berries like rose-hips, which were sour and flavorless, but which eased hunger a little.

The next day was dreadful, forcing their way through the thinning underbrush, but they halted early, and Kennard, turning to Larry, said, "Give me your handkerchief."

Obediently, Larry handed it over. It was crumpled and filthy, and he couldn't imagine what Kennard wanted it for, but he sat and watched Kennard rip it into tiny strips and knot them until he had a fairly long strip of twisted cloth. He searched, on silent feet, till he found a hole in the ground; then, bending

109

a branch low, rigged a noose and snare. He motioned to Larry to lie flat and still, following suit himself. It seemed hours that they lay there silent, Larry's body growing cramped and stiff, and Kennard turning angry eyes on him when he ventured to ease a sore muscle by moving it ever so slightly.

A long time later, some small animal poked an inquisitive snout from the hole; instantly, Kennard jerked the noose tight and the small creature kicked, writhing, in the air.

Larry winced, then reflected that, after all, he had been eating meat all his life and this was no time to get squeamish. He watched, feeling vaguely useless and superfluous, as Kennard wrung the creature's neck, skinned and gutted it, and gathered dead twigs for a fire.

"It would be safer not to," he said, with a wry smile, "but I haven't any taste for raw meat – and if they're still on our trail after this long, we're out of luck anyhow."

The small furred thing was not much bigger than a rabbit; they finished every scrap of the meat and gnawed the bones. Kennard insisted on himself covering the fire and scraping leaves over the place where it had been, so that no sign of their camp remained.

When they slept that night, Larry lay long awake, feeling somehow ill at ease; half envying Kennard's woodcraft – he was lost and helpless in these woods without the other boy's knowledge – yet possessed by a nagging disquiet that had nothing to do with that. The woods were filled with strange noises, the far-away cries of night birds and the padding of strange beasts, and Larry tried to tell himself that he was simply uneasy about the strangeness of it all. The next morning when they prepared to go on, he kept glancing around until Kennard noticed and asked him, rather irritably, what was the matter.

"I keep hearing – and not quite seeing – things," Larry said reluctantly.

"Imagination," Kennard said, shrugging it off, but Larry's disquiet persisted.

That day was much like the former. They struggled down exhausting slopes, forcing their way through brushwood; they scrambled through country that looked like smooth forest but was matted with dead trees and deep ravines.

At night Kennard snared a bird and was about to light a fire to cook it when he noticed Larry's disquiet.

"Whatever is the matter with you?"

Larry could only shake his head, silently. He knew – without knowing *how* he knew – that Kennard *must not* light that fire, and it seemed so senseless that he was ready to cry with the tension of it. Kennard regarded him with a look halfway between impatience and pity.

"You're worn out, that's what's the matter," he said, "and for all I know you're still half-poisoned by the drug they gave you. Why don't you lie down and have a sleep? Rest and food will help you more than anything else." He took out his tinderbox and began to strike the fire –

Larry cried out, an inarticulate sound, and leaped to grab his wrist, spilling tinder. Kennard, in a rage, dropped the box and struck Larry, hard across the face.

"Damn you, look what you've made me do!"

"I – " Larry's voice failed. He could not even resent the blow. "I don't know why I did that."

Kennard stood over him, fury slowly giving way to puzzlement and pity. "You're out of your head. Pick up that tinder – " When Larry had obeyed, he stood back, warily. "Am I going to have trouble with you, damn it, or do we have to eat raw meat?"

Larry dropped to the ground and buried his face in his hands. The reluctant spark caught the tinder; Kennard knelt, coaxing the tiny spark into flame, feeding it with twigs. Larry sat motionless, even the smell of the roasting meat unable to penetrate through the thick, growing fog of distress. He did not see Kennard looking at him with a frown of growing dismay. When Kennard took the roasted bird from the fire and broke it in half, Larry only shook his head. He was famished, the smell of the meat made his mouth water and his eyes sting, but the fear, like a thick miasma around him, fogged away everything else. He hardly heard Kennard speak. He took the meat the Darkovan boy put into his hands, and put it into his mouth, but he could neither chew nor swallow. At last he heard Kennard say, gently, "All right. Later, maybe, you'll want it." But the words sounded very far away through the thing that was thickening, growing in him. He could feel Kennard's thoughts,

111

like seeing the glow of sparks through half-dead ash; Kennard thought that he, Larry, was losing his grip on reality. Larry didn't blame him. He thought so too. But the knowledge could not break through the numbing fear that grew and grew –

It broke, suddenly, a great cresting wave. He heard himself cry out, in alarm, and spring upright, but it was too late.

Suddenly the clearing was alive with darkly clustering swarms of crouching figures. Kennard yelled and leaped to his feet, but they were already struggling in the meshes of a great net of twisted vines that had jerked them closely together.

The fogged thickness of apprehension was gone, and Larry was clear headed, alert, aware of this new captivity. The net had drawn them close, but not off their feet; they could see the forms around them clearly in the firelight and the color of phosphorescent torches of some sort. And the new attackers were not human.

They were formed like men, though smaller; furred, naked save for bands of leaves or some woven matting around their waists; with great pinkish eyes and long prehensile fingers and toes. They clustered around the net, twittering in high, birdlike speech. Larry glanced curiously at Kennard, and the other lad said tersely. "Trailmen. Nonhumans. They live in the trees. I didn't know they'd ever come this far to the south. The fire probably drew them. If I'd known – " He glanced ruefully at their dying fire. The trailmen were circling round it, shrilling, poking at it gingerly with long sticks, throwing dirt at it, and finally they managed to cover it entirely. Then they stamped on it with what looked like glee, dancing a sort of victory dance, and finally one of the creatures came to the net and delivered a long speech in their shrill language; neither of the boys, of course, could understand a word, but it sounded enraged and triumphant.

Kennard said, "They're terrified of fire, and they hate humans because we use it. They're afraid of forest fire, of course. To them, fire means death."

"What are they going to do to us?"

"I don't know." Kennard looked at Larry curiously, but all he said, at last, was, "Next time I'll trust your hunches. Evidently you have some precognition too, as well as telepathy."

To Larry, the trailmen looked like big monkeys – or like the *kyrri*, only smaller and without the immense dignity of those other creatures. He hoped they did not also have the *kyrri* trick of giving off electric sparks!

Evidently they did not. They drew the net tight around the boys' feet, forcing them to walk by tugging at the vine ropes, but offered no further violence. A few hundred feet of this, and they came upon a widened path; Kennard whistled, softly, at sight of it.

"We've been in trailmen country, evidently, most of the day. Probably they've been watching us all day, but they might not have bothered us if I hadn't lit that fire. I ought to have known."

It was easier to walk on the cleared path. Larry had lost track of time, but was stumbling with weariness when, much later, they came to a broad clearing, lighted by phosphorescence which, he now saw, came from fungus growing on broad trees. After a discussion in their twittering speech, the trailmen looped the net-ropes around the nearest tree and began to swarm up the trunk of the next.

"I wonder if they're just going to leave us here?" Kennard muttered.

A hard jerk on the rope disabused them. Slowly, the net began to rise, jerking them off their feet, so that they hung up, swaying, in the great bag. Kennard shouted in protest, and Larry yelled, but evidently the trailmen were taking no chances. Once the slow motion rise stopped, and Larry wondered if they were going to be hung up here in a sack like a pair of big sausages; but after a heart-stopping interval, they began to rise again.

Kennard swore, in a smothered voice. "I should have cut our way out, the minute they left us!" He drew his dagger and began feverishly to saw at one of the great vines enclosing them. Larry caught his arm.

"No, Kennard. We'd only fall." He pointed downward into the dizzying distance. "And if they see that, they'll only take the knife from you. Hide it! Hide it!"

Kennard, realizing the truth of what Larry said, thrust the knife into his shirt. The lads clung together as the great vine net ascended higher and higher toward the treetops; far from wishing, now, to cut their way out, they feared it would break.

113

The light brightened as they neared the lower branches of the immense trees, and at last, with a bump that flung them against one another, the net was hauled up over a branch and on to the floor of the trailmen's encampment in the trees.

Larry said urgently, "One of us should be a match for any two of those little creatures! Perhaps we can fight our way free."

But the swarms of trailmen surrounding them put a stop to Larry's optimism. There must have been forty or fifty, men, women and a few small pale-fuzzed babies. At least a dozen of the men rushed at the net, bearing Larry and Kennard along with them. When, however, they ceased struggling and made signs that they would walk peacefully, one of the trailmen – he had a lean, furred monkeyface and green, intelligent eyes – came forward and began to unfasten the complicated knots of the snare with his prehensile competent fingers. The trailmen, however, were taking no chances on a sudden rush; they surrounded the two boys closely, ringing them round and giving them no chance to escape. Seeing for the moment that escape was impossible, Larry looked round, studying the strange world of the trail-city around him.

Between the tops of a circle of great trees, a floor had been constructed of huge hewn logs, covered over with what looked like woven rush-matting. It swayed, slightly and disconcertingly, with every movement and step; but Larry, seeing that it supported this huge shifting crowd of trailmen, realized that it must have been constructed in such a way as to support immense weights. How could so simple a people have figured out such a feat of engineering? Well, he supposed that if beavers could make dams that challenged the ingenuity of human engineers, these nonhumans could do just about the equivalent in the treetops.

A pale greenish light filtered in from the leaves overhead; by this dim light he saw a circle of huts constructed at the edges of the flooring. A thatch of green growing leaves had been trained over their roofs, and vines covered their edges, hung with clusters of grapes so succulent and delicious that Larry realized that he was parched.

They were thrust into one of the huts; a tough grating slammed down behind them, and they were prisoners.

Prisoners of the trailmen!

Larry slumped on the floor, wearily. "Out of the frying pan into the fire," he remarked, and at Kennard's puzzled look repeated the remark in rough-hewn Darkovan. Kennard smiled wryly. "We have a similar saying: 'The game that walks from the trap to the cookpot.'"

Kennard hauled out his knife and began tentatively to saw at the material of the vines comprising their prison. No use – the vines were green and tough, thickly knotted and twined, and resisted the knife as if they had been iron bars. After a long grimace, he put the knife away and sat staring gloomily at the moss-implanted floor of the hut.

Hours dragged by. They heard the distant shrill and twittering voices of the trailmen, birdsongs in the treetops, the strident sound of cricketlike insects. In the moss that grew on the hut floor there were numerous small insects that chirped and thrust inquisitive heads up, without fear, like house pets, at the two boys.

Gradually the green-filtered light dimmed; it grew colder and darker, and finally wholly dark; the noises quieted, and around them the trail-city slept. They sat in darkness, Larry thinking with an almost anguished nostalgia of the clean quiet world of the Terran Trade City. Why had he ever wanted to leave it?

There, there would be lights and sounds, food and company, people speaking his own tongue . . .

In the darkness Kennard stirred, mumbled something unintelligible and slept again, exhausted. Larry felt suddenly ashamed of his thoughts. His quest for adventure had led him here, against all warnings – and Kennard seemed likely to share whatever obscure fate was in store for them at the hands of the trailmen. By Darkovan standards he, Larry, was a man. He could at least behave like one. He found the warmest corner of the hut, hauled off his boots and his jacket, and, on an impulse, spread his jacket over the sleeping Kennard; then, curled himself up on the moss, he slept.

He slept heavily and long; when he woke, Kennard was tugging at his sleeve and the wicker-woven door was opening. It opened, however, only a little way; a wooden tray was shoved inside and the door closed again quickly. From outside they heard the bar drop into place.

It was light, and warmer. With one impulse, the two boys fell

115

on the tray. It was piled high with food; the luscious grapes they had seen growing, nuts with soft shells which Larry managed to open with the broken blade of his small knife, some soft, spongy, earthy things which smelled like excellent honey. They made a substantial meal, then put the tray down and looked at one another, neither wanting to be the first to speak of the apparent hopelessness of their position.

Larry spoke first examining the intricate carving of the tray: "They have tools?"

"Oh, yes. Very fine flint knives – I've seen them in a museum of non-human artifacts in Arilinn," Kennard returned, "and some of the mountain people trade with them – give them knives and tools in return for certain things they grow: dye-stuffs, mostly, certain herbs for medicines. Nuts and fruits. That sort of thing."

"They seem to have a fairly complex culture of their own, then."

"They do. But they fear and hate men, probably because we use fire."

Larry, thinking of the forest fire – only a few days ago – could not really blame the trailmen for their fears. He examined the cup which had contained the honey. It was made of unfired clay, sun-baked and rough. What else could a culture do without fire?

There were still some fruits and nuts remaining on the tray, so abundant had been the meal. He said, "I hope they're not fattening us up for their Sunday dinner."

Kennard laughed faintly. "No. They don't even eat animals. They're completely vegetarian as far as I ever heard."

Larry exploded. "Then what the mischief do they want with us?"

Kennard shrugged. "I don't know – and I'm damned if I know how to ask them!"

Larry was silent, thinking that over. Then: "Aren't you a telepath?"

"Not a good one. Anyway, telepathy transmits worded thoughts, as a rule – and emotions. Two telepaths who don't speak the same language have such different concepts that it's almost impossible to read one another's minds. And trying to read the mind of a non-human – well, a highly skilled

116

Hasturlord, or a *leronis* (a sorceress like the one you saw at the fire) might be able to manage it. I couldn't even try it."

So, that, it seemed, was that.

The day dragged by. No one came near them. At evening, another tray piled high with fruit, nuts and mushrooms was slid into their prison, and the old one deftly extracted. Still a third day came and went, with neither of the boys able to imagine a way to get out of their predicament. Their jailer entered their hut, now to give them food and take away their empty dishes. He was a large and powerful creature – for a trailman – but walked with a limp. He seemed friendly but wary. Kennard and Larry discussed the possibility of overpowering the creature and making their escape, but that would only land them in the trailmen's city – with, perhaps, hundreds of miles of trailmen's forest country to be traversed. So they contented themselves with discussing plan after futile plan. None of them seemed even remotely feasible.

It seemed, by the growing light, to be noon of the fourth day when the door of their prison opened and three trailmen entered, escorting a fourth who seemed, from their air of deference, to be a person of some importance among them. Like the others, he was naked save for the belt of leaves about his waist, but he wore a string of clay beads mingled with crimson berries, and had an air of indefinable dignity which made Larry, for some reason think of Lorill Hastur.

He bowed slightly and remarked in perfectly understandable, though somewhat shrill Darkovan dialect: "Good morning. I trust you are comfortable and that you have not been harmed?"

Both boys leaped to their feet as if electrified. He spoke an understandable tongue! The guards surrounding the trailman personage put their hands to their flint knives, but seeing that neither boy made a move toward the man, stood back.

Kennard shouted, "Comfortable be damned! What the mischief do you mean by keeping us here anyhow!"

The trailmen murmured, twittering, in shock and dismay, and the Personage spun on his heel in obvious offense; Kennard instantly changed his tactics. He bowed deeply.

"Forgive me. I" – he looked wildly at Larry – "I spoke in haste. We – "

117

Larry said, speaking the same dialect, "We have been well fed and kept out of the rain, if that is what you mean, sir." The word he used would also have been translated "Your honor." "But would your very high honor condescend to explain to us why we are being taken from our road and put in this exceptionally damp and confining place at all?"

The trailman's face was stern. He said, "Your people burn down the woods with the red-thing-that-eats-the-woods. Animals die. Trees perish. You were being watched and when you built the red-thing-that-eats-the-woods, we seized you."

"Then will you let us go again?" Kennard asked.

The trailman slowly made a negative gesture. "We have one protection, and only one, against the red-thing-that-eats-the-woods. Whenever your people come over into the country of the People of the Sky, they never leave it again. So that your people will fear coming into our world, and there will be no fear of the red-thing-that-eats-the-woods destroying more of our cities."

Kennard with a furious gesture, rolled back his sleeves. There were still crimson burn scars on them. "Listen, you – " he began; and with an effort, amended, "Hear me, your – your High Muchness. Just a few days ago, I and my family and my friends spent many, many days putting out a fire. It is not *my* kind of people who burn down woods We are – we are running away from the evil kind of people who set fires to burn down woods."

"Then why were you building a – you call it *fire?*"

"To cook our food."

The trailman's face was severe. "And your kind of – of *man*" – the word was one of inexpressible contempt on his lips – "eats of our brothers-that-have-life!"

"Ways differ and customs differ," said Kennard doggedly, "but we will not burn down your woods. We will even promise not to build a fire while we are in your woods, if you will let us go."

"You are of the fire-making kind. We will not let you go. I have spoken."

He turned on his heel and walked out. Behind him, his guards stalked out, and the bolt fell into place.

"And that," said Kennard, "is very much *that*."

He sat down, chin in hands, and stared grimly into space.

Larry was also feeling despair. Obviously the trailmen would not harm them. Equally obviously, however, they seemed likely to be sitting here in this prison – well fed, well housed, but caged like alien horrid animals – until hell froze over, as far as the Personage was concerned.

He found himself thinking in terms of the trailmen's way of life. If you depended on the woods for very life, fire was your worst fear – and evidently, to them, fire was a wild thing that could never be controlled. He remembered their triumphant dance of joy when they had managed to put out Kennard's little cookfire.

He said thoughtfully, "You still have your flint and tinder, don't you?"

Kennard caught him up instantly. "Right! We can burn our way out with torches, and no one will dare to come near us."

Suddenly his face fell. "No. There is a danger that their city might catch fire. We would be wiping out a whole village of perfectly harmless creatures."

And Larry followed his thought. Better to sit here in prison indefinitely – after all, they were being well fed and kindly treated – than risk exterminating a whole village of these absolutely harmless little people. People who would not even kill a rabbit for food. Sooner or later they would find a way out. Until then, they would not risk harming the trailmen, who had not harmed them.

They were interrupted by the entry of their guard, limping heavily, carrying a tray of their food – the nuts, the honey, and what looked like birds' eggs. Larry made a face – raw eggs? Well, he supposed they were a treat to the trailmen, and they were at least giving their prisoner-guests of their best. But a boiled egg would be a pleasant enough meal.

Kennard was asking the trailman, by signs, how he had hurt his leg. The trailman sprang into a crouch, his head laid into a feral gesture; he actually looked like the great carnivore he was imitating. He made a brutal clawing gesture; he fell to the mossy floor of the hut, doubled up, imitating great pain; then displayed the cruelly festering wound. Larry turned sick at the sight of it; the thigh was swollen to nearly twice its size, and greenish pus was oozing from the wound. The trailman made

119

a stoical shrug, pointed to his flint knife, gestured, struggled like a man being held down, hopped like a man with one leg, folded his hands, closed his eyes, held his breath like a man dead. He picked up the tray and hobbled out.

Kennard, his face twisting, shook his head. "I suppose you got all that? He means they'll have to cut his leg off soon or he will die."

"And it's so damned unnecessary!" Larry said violently. "All it needs it lancing and antibiotics, and a little sterile care – " Suddenly, he started.

"Kennard! That pot they brought the honey in, do you still have it?"

"Yes."

"I'm no good at making a fire with flint and tinder. But can you make one? A very small one in the pot? Enough, say, to sterilize a knife? To heat water very hot?"

"What do you – "

"I have an idea," Larry said between his teeth, "and it just might work." He pulled his medical kit from his pocket. "I have some antiseptic powder, and antibiotics. Not much. But probably enough, considering that the fellow must have the constitution of – of one of these trees, to live through a clawing like that and still be walking around at all."

"Larry, if we kindle a fire they will probably kill us."

"So we keep it in the pot, covered. The old fellow looks intelligent – the one who spoke Darkovan. If we show him that it can't possibly get out of a clay pot – "

Kennard caught his thought. "Zandru's hells, it just might work, Larry! But, Gods above, are you then apprenticed to be a curer-of-wounds among your people, like my cousin Dyan Ardais?"

"No. This knowledge is as common with the boys of my people as – " he sought wildly for a simile, and Kennard, following his thought as usual, suppled one: "As the knowledge of sword-play among mine?"

Larry nodded. He took over then, giving instructions: "If the chap yells, we'll be swamped, and never have a chance to finish. So you and I will jump him and keep him from getting one squeak out. Then you sit on him while I fix up his leg. We'll get just one chance to keep him from yelling – so don't muff it!"

120

By evening their preparations were made. The light was poor, and Larry fretted; though the light from the fire-pot helped a little. They waited, breathless. Had their jailer been changed, had he died of his terrible wound? No, after a time they heard his characteristic halting step. The door opened.

He saw the pot and the fire. He opened his mouth to scream.

But the scream never got out. Kennard's arm was across his throat, and a crude, improvised gag of a strip torn from Larry's shirt-tail was stuffed into his mouth. Larry felt slightly sick. He knew what must be done, but had never done anything even remotely like it before. He held the knife in the fire until it glowed red-hot, then let it cool somewhat, and, setting his teeth, made a long gash in the swollen, festering leg.

There was an immediate gush of greenish, stinking matter from the wound. Larry sponged it away. It seemed there was no end to the stuff that oozed from the wound, and it was a sickening business, but finally the stuff was tinged with blood and he could see clean flesh below.

He sponged it repeatedly with the hot water heated in the second pot; when it was as clean as he could make it, he sprinkled the antibiotic powder into the wound, covered it with the cleanest piece of cloth he had – a fragment of bandage remaining in the medical kit – and took the gag from the man's mouth.

The man had long since ceased to struggle. He lay blinking in stuporous surprise, looking down at his leg, which now had only a clean gash. Suddenly he rose, bowed half a dozen times profoundly to the boys, and backed out of the room.

Larry slumped on the floor, exhausted. He wondered suddenly if what he had done had really endangered their lives. The trailmen's customs were so differernt from theirs, there was really no way of telling; they might consider this just as evil as killing a rabbit.

After a while, at Kennard's urging, he sat up and ate some supper. He needed it – even if he had the feeling that he might be eating his last meal. They fed the small fire with fragments of vine from the dead leaves, and toasted their mushrooms over it. For a while they felt almost festive. Much later, they heard steps, and looked at one another, with no need for words.

121

This is it. Life or death?

Kennard said nothing, but reached silently for Larry's hand; he clasped it and the clasp slid up Larry's elbow until their arms were enlaced as well as their hands. Unfamiliar as the gesture was, Larry knew it was a sign not alone of friendship but of affection and tenderness. He felt faintly embarrassed, but he said, in a low voice, "If it's bad news – I'm sorry as hell I got you into this – but it's been damn nice knowing you."

An instant before the door opened, Larry saw it, a clear flash of awareness; the sight of the trailman chief, and his face was grave, but he was alone, and unweaponed. It was not, at any rate, instant death.

The trailman said, "I have seen what you did for Rhhomi. I cannot believe that you are evil men. Yet you are of the kind who make fire." With a sort of grave dignity, he seated himself. "None is so young he cannot teach, or so old he cannot learn. Am I to learn from you, strange men?"

Kennard said swiftly, "We have told you already that we have no will to harm even the least of your people or creatures, Honorable One."

"Yes." But it was at Larry that the trailman chief looked. He said, irrelevantly, it seemed, "Among my folk my title is Old One, and what is age if not wisdom? Have you wisdom for me, son of a strange land?"

Larry reached behind him for the honey pot, containing still a few glowing embers of fire. The Old One shrank, but controlled himself with an effort. Larry tried to speak his simplest Darkovan; after all, the language was strange to both himself and this alien creature.

"It is harmless here," he said, searching for words. "See, the walls of your clay pot keep it harmless so that it cannot burn. If you feed it with – with dead twigs and little bits of dead, dry wood, it will serve you and not hurt you."

The Old One reached out, evidently conquering an ingrained shrinking, and touched the pot. He said, "Then it can be servant and not master?

"And a knife made clean in this fire will heal?"

"Yes," said Larry, bypassing the whole of germ theory, "or a wound washed with water made very hot, will heal better than a dirty wound."

122

The Old One rose, bearing the firepot in his hands. He said, gravely, "For this gift, then, of healing, my people thank you. And as a sign of this, be under our protection within our woods. Wear this" – and he extended two garlands of yellow flowers – "and none of our people will harm you. But build no red-flames-to-eat-our-woods within the limits of these branches."

Larry, sensing that the Old One spoke to him, said gravely, "You have my pledge."

The Old One threw open the door of the hut.

"Be free to go."

Awkwardly they settled the crowns of yellow flowers over their heads. The trailmen surged backward as the Old One came forth, bearing in his hands the pot of fire. He said ceremoniously, handing it to a woman. "I place this thing in your hands. You and your daughters and the daughters of your daughters are to feed it and bear responsibility that it does not escape."

The scene had a grave solemnity that made Larry, for some reason – perhaps only relief – want to giggle. But he kept his gravity, while they were escorted to the edge of the trailmen's village, shown a long ladder down which they could climb, and finally, with infinite relief, set foot again on the green and solid ground.

X

All that day they walked, through the trails of the forest. Now and again, from the corner of their eyes, they caught a glimpse of movement, but they saw not a sign of a trailman. They slept that night hearing sounds overhead, but now without fear, knowing that the yellow garlands would protect them in trailman country.

So far neither of them had spoken of their escape. There was no need for words between them now. But when, on the second day – a day clouded and sunless, with a promise of rain – they sat to eat their meal of berries and the odd fungus the trailmen had shown them, which grew plentifully along these paths, Kennard finally spoke.

"You know, of course, that there will be fires. Houses will burn. Maybe even woods will burn. They're not human."

"I'm not so sure," Larry said thoughtfully. "Among the Terrans, they would be called at least humanoid. They have a culture."

"Yet was it safe to give them fire? I would never have dared," Kennard said, "not if we died there. For more centuries than I can count, man and nonhuman have lived together on Darkover in a certain balance. And now, with the trailmen using fire – " He shrugged, helplessly, and Larry suddenly began to see the implications of what he had done. "Still," he said stubbornly, "they'll learn. They'll make mistakes, there will be mis-uses, but they will learn. Their pottery will improve as it is fired. They will, perhaps, learn to cook food. They will grow and develop. Nothing remains static," he said. He repeated the Terran creed, "A civilization changes – or it dies."

Kennard's face flushed in sudden, sullen anger, and Larry, realizing that for the first time since his rescue they were conscious of being alien to one another, knew something else. Kennard was jealous. He had been the rescuer, the leader. Yet Larry had saved them, where Kennard would have given up because he feared change. Larry had taken command – and Kennard, second place.

"That is the Terran way," Kennard said sullenly. "Change. For better or worse, but change. No matter how good a thing is – change it, just for the sake of change."

Larry, with a growing wisdom, was silent. It was, he knew, a deeper conflict than they could ever resolve with words alone; a whole civilization based on expansion and growth, pitted against one based on tradition. He felt like saying, "Anyhow, we're alive," but forbore. Kennard had saved his life many times over. It hardly would become him to boast about beginning to even the score.

That evening they came to the edge of the trailmen's rain forest and into the open foothills again – bare, trackless hills, unexplored, rocky, covered with scrubby brush and low, bunchy grass. Beyond them lay the mountain ranges, and beyond that –

"There lies the pass," Kennard said, "and beyond it lies Hastur country, and the home of Castle Hastur. We're within sight of home." He sounded hopeful, even joyous, but Larry heard the trembling in his voice. Before them lay miles of canyons and gullies, without road or track or path, and beyond that lay the high mountain pass. The day was dim and sunless, the peaks in shadow, but even at this distance Larry could see that snow lay in their depths.

"How far?"

"Four days travel, perhaps, if it were open prairie or forest," Kennard said. "Or one day's ride on a swift horse, if any horse could travel these infernal arroyos."

He stood frowning, gazing down into the mazelike network of canyons. "The worst of it is, the sun is clouded, and I find it hard to calculate the path we must follow. From here to the pass we must travel due westward. But with the sun in shadow – " He knelt momentarily, and Larry, wondering if he were praying, saw that instead he was examining the very faint shadow cast by the clouded sun. Finally he said, "As long as we can see the mountain peak, we need only follow it. I suppose" – he rose, shrugging wearily – "we may as well begin."

He set off downward into one of the canyons. Larry, envying him his show of confidence, stumbled after him. He was weary and footsore, and hungry, but he would not show himself less manly than Kennard.

All that day and all the next they stumbled and scrambled among the thorny, rocky slopes of the barren foothills. They went in no danger of hunger, for the bushes, so thorny and barren in appearance, were lush with succulent berries and ripening nuts. That evening Kennard snared several small birds who were feeding fearlessly on their abundance. They were out of trailmen country now, so that they dared to make fire; and it seemed to Larry that no festive dinner had ever tasted so good as the flesh of these nutty birds, roasted over their small fire and eaten half-raw and without salt. Kennard said, as they sat companionably munching drumsticks, "This place is a hunter's paradise! The birds are without fear."

"And good eating," Larry commented, cracking a bone for the succulent marrow.

"It's even possible that we might meet a hunting party," Kennard said hopefully. "Perhaps some of the men from the Hastur country beyond the mountains hunt here – where the game roams in such abundance."

But they were both silent at the corollary of that statement. If no one hunted here, where the hunting was so splendid, then the mountain pass that lay between them and safety must be fearsome indeed!

The third day was cloudier than the last, and Kennard stopped often to examine the fainter and fainter shadows and calculate the sun's position by them. The land was rising now; the gullies were steeper and more thorny, the slopes harder to scramble up. Toward that evening a thin, fine drizzle began to fall, and even Kennard, with all his skill, could not build a fire. They gnawed cold roast meat from the night before, and dampish fruits, and slept huddled together for warmth in a rock-lined crevasse.

All the next day the rain drizzled down, thin and pale, and the purplish light held no hint of sun or shadow. Larry, watching Kennard grow ever more silent and tense, could

126

not at last contain his anxiety. He said, "Kennard, we're lost. I know we're going the wrong way. Look, the land slopes downhill, and we have to keep going upward toward the mountains."

"I know we're going downhill, muffin-head," snapped Kennard, "into this canyon. On the other side the land rises higher. Can't you see?"

"With this rain I can't see a thing," said Larry honestly, "and what's more, I don't think you can either."

Kennard rounded on him, suddenly furious: "I suppose you think you could do better?"

"I didn't say that," Larry protested, but Kennard was tensely trying to find a shadow. It seemed completely hopeless. They were not even sure of the time of day, so that even the position of the sun would have been no help, could they have seen a shadow; this damp, darkish drizzle made no distinction between early afternoon and deep twilight.

He heard Kennard murmur, almost in despair, "If I could only get a sight of the mountain peak!"

It was the first time the Darkovan boy had sounded despair, and Larry felt the need to comfort and reassure. He said, "Kennard, it's not as bad as all that. We won't starve here. Sooner or later the sun will shine, or the rain will stop, and the pass will be before us clearly. Then any one of these little hilltops will show us our right direction. Why don't we find a sheltered place and just wait out the rainstorm?"

He had not expected instant agreement, but he was not prepared for the violence, the fury with which the Darkovan boy rounded on him.

"You damned, infernal, bumbling idiot," he shouted, "what do you *think* I'd do if it was only me? Do you think I can't have sense enough to do what any ten-year-old with sense enough to tie his own bootlaces would do in such a storm? But with you – "

"I don't understand – "

"You wouldn't," shouted Kennard. "You never understand anything, you damned – *Terranan!*" For the first time in all their friendship, the word on his lips was an insult. Larry felt his blood rise high in return. Kennard had saved his life; but there was a point beyond which he could not rub it in any further.

"If I have so little sense – ?"

"Listen," Kennard said, with suppressed violence, "my father gave his surety to the *Terranan* lords for your safety. Do you think you can simply disappear? Your damned Terrans who can never let any man live his own life or die his own death? No, damn it. If you visit my people – and you vanish and are killed – do you suppose the Terrans will ever believe it was accident and not a deep-laid plot? You headblind Terrans without even telepathy enough to know when a man speaks truth, so that your fumbling insolent idiots of people dared – they *dared*! – to doubt that my father, a lord of the Comyn and of the Seven Domains, spoke truth?

"It's true, I rescued you for my own honor and because we had sworn friendship. But also because, unless I brought you safely back to your people, your damned Terrans will be poking and prying, searching and avenging!" He stopped. He had to. He was completely out of breath after his outburst, his face red with fury, his eyes blazing, and Larry, in sudden terror, felt the other's rage as a murderous, almost a deadly thing. He realized suddenly that he stood very close to death at that moment. The fury of an unleashed telepath – and one too young to have control over his power – beat on Larry with a surge of power like a ship. It rolled over him like a crashing surf. It pounded him physically to his knees.

He bent before it. And then, as suddenly as it had come, he realized that he had strength to meet it. He raised his eyes gravely to Kennard and said aloud, "Look, my friend" – (he used the word *bredu*) " – I did not know this. I did not make my people's laws, no more than you caused the feud that set the bandits on our hunting party." And he was amazed at the steady force with which he countered the furious assault of rage.

Slowly, Kennard quieted. Larry felt the red surges of Kennard's fury receding, until at last the Darkovan boy stood before him silent, just a kid again and a scared one. He didn't apologize, but Larry didn't expect him to. He said simply, "So it's a matter of time, you see, Lerrys." The Darkovan form of Larry's name was, Larry knew, tacit apology. "And as you

128

care for your people, I care for my father. And this is the first day of the rainy season. I had hoped to be out of these hills, and through the passes, before this. We were delayed by the trailmen, or we should be safe now, and a message of your safety on its way to your father. If I had the starstone still – " he was silent, then shrugged. "Well, that is the Comyn law." He drew a deep breath. "Now, which way did you say you thought was west?"

"I didn't say," Larry said, honestly. He did not know until much later just how rare a thing he had done; he had faced the unleashed wrath of an Alton and a telepath – and been unharmed. Later, he remembered it and shook in his shoes; but now he just felt relieved that Kennard had calmed down.

"But," he said, "there's no point in going in circles. All these canyons look exactly alike to me. If we had a compass – " He broke off. He began to search frantically in his pockets. The bandits had not taken it from him because the main blade was broken. The trailmen had not even seen it. As a weapon it was worthless. He had not even been able to use it to help Kennard clean and gut the birds they had eaten.

But it had a magnetized blade!

And a magnetized blade, properly used, could make an improvised compass . . .

The first turn-out of his pockets failed to find it; then he remembered that during their time with the trailmen, fearing they might regard any tool, however small, as a weapon, he had thrust it into his medical kit. He took it out, and snapped the magnetized blade off against a stone, then tested it against the metal of the broken main blade. It retained its magnetism. Now if he could only remember how it was done. It had been a footnote in one of his mathematics texts in childhood, half forgotten. Kennard, meanwhile, watched as if Larry's brain had snapped, while Larry experimented with a bit of string and finally, looking at Kennard's long, square-cut hair, demanded, "Give me one of your hairs."

"Are you out of your wits?"

"No," Larry said, "I think I may be *in* them, at last. I should have thought of this from the beginning. If I could have taken a bearing when the sun was still shining, and we had a clear view of the pass ahead of us, I'd know – ”

Without raising his head, he accepted the hair which Kennard gave him gingerly, as if he were humoring a lunatic. He knotted the hair around the magnetized blade and waited. The blade was tiny and light, hardly bigger than the needles which had been the first improvised compasses. It swung wildly for a few moments; stopped.

“What superstitious rigmarole – ” Kennard began, stopped. “You must have something on your mind,” he conceded, “but what?”

Larry began to explain the theory by which the magnetic compass worked; Kennard cut him short.

“Everyone knows that a certain kind of metal – you call it a magnet – will attract metal. But how can this help us?”

For a moment Larry despaired. He had forgotten the level of Darkovan technology – or lack of it – and how could he, in one easy lesson, explain the two magnetic poles of a planet, the theory of the magnetic compass which pointed to the true pole at all times, the manner of taking a compass direction and following? He started, but he was making very heavy weather of explaining the magnetic field around a planet. To begin with, he simply did not have the technological vocabulary in Darkovan – if there was one, which he doubted. He was reminded of the trailman chief calling fire “the red thing which eats the woods.” He felt like that while he tried to explain about iron filings and magnetic currents. Finally he gave up, holding the improvised compass in one hand.

He said helplessly, “Kennard, I can't explain it to you any more than you can explain to me how you destroyed that blue jewel of yours – or how your psychics herded a batch of clouds across the sky to put out a fire. But I helped you do it, didn't I? And it worked? We can't possibly be any worse off than we are already, can we? And the Terran ships find their way between the stars by using this kind of – of science. So will you at least let me *try*?”

Kennard was silent for a moment. At last he said, “I suppose you are right. We could not be worse off.”

Larry knelt and drew an improvised sketch map on the ground, what he remembered of the mountain range he had seen from the distance. "Now here's the mountains and here is the edge of the trailmen's forest. How far had we come before you lost sure sight of exactly where we were going?"

Hesitantly, with many frowns and rememberings, Kennard traced out a route.

"And that was – exactly how long ago? Try to be as accurate as you can, Kennard; how many miles ago did you begin not to be absolutely sure?"

Kennard put his finger on the improvised map.

"So we're within about five hours walk from that point." He drew a circle around the point Kennard had shown as their last positive location. "We could be anywhere in this circle, but if we keep west and keep going west we'll have to hit the mountains – we can't possibly miss them." He tried not to think of what would lie before them then. Kennard thought of it as just the final hurdle, but the journey with the bandits through their own dreadful chasms and crags – bound and handcuffed like sacked luggage – had given him an enduring horror of the Darkovan mountains that was to last his lifetime.

"If this works . . ." Kennard said, skeptically, but immediately looked an apology. "What do I have to do first? Is there any specific ritual for the use of this – this amulet?"

Larry, by main force, held back a shout of half-hysterical laughter. Instead, he said gravely, "Just cross your fingers that it will work," and started questioning Kennard about the minor discrepancies, of the seasons, and the sun's rising and setting. Darkover – he knew from its extremes of climate – must be a planet with an exaggeratedly tilted axis, and he would have to figure out just how far north or south of true west the sun set at this season of the year in this latitude. How he blessed the teacher at Quarters B who had loaned him the book on Darkover geography – otherwise he might not even have been sure whether they were in the southern, rather than the northern hemisphere. He boggled at the thought of trying to explain an equator to Kennard.

A degree or two wouldn't matter – not with a range of mountains hundreds of miles long, that they couldn't miss if they tried – but the nearer they came out to the pass itself, the sooner they would be home. And the sooner Kennard's father

131

would be out of trouble. He was amazed at how responsible he felt.

The compass would steady, he realized, if he let it swing freely without his hand moving. All they had to do was take a rough bearing, follow it, checking it again and again every few miles.

Once again, he realized, he had taken the lead in the expedition, and Kennard, reluctantly, was forced to follow. It bothered him, and he knew Kennard didn't like it. He hoped, at least, that it wouldn't bring on another outburst of rage.

He stood up, looking at the muddy mess of their improvised map. He was cold and drenched, but he assumed an air of confidence which, in reality, he was far from feeling.

"Well, if we're going to risk it," he said, "west is that way. So let's start walking. I'm ready if you are."

It was hard, slow going, scrambling into canyons and up slopes, stopping every hour to swing the compass free and wait for it to steady and point, re-drawing the improvised compass card in the mud. Larry finally shortened this step by drawing one on a page of his battered notebook. The rain went on, remorselessly, not hard, never soaking, but always *there* – a thin, fine, chilling drizzle that eventually seemed worse than the worst and hardest downpour. His arm, the one the bandits had harnessed behind his back, felt both numb and sore, but there wasn't a thing he could do but set his teeth and try to think about something else. That night they literally dug themselves into a bank of dead leaves, in a vain attempt to keep some of the worst of the rain off. Their clothes were wet. The food they munched was wet – berries, nuts, fruits and a sort of root like a raw potato. Kennard could easily enough have snared small game, but they tacitly agreed that even cold raw sour berries and mushrooms were preferable to raw wet meat. And Kennard swore that in this drizzle, at this season, in this kind of country, not even a *kyrri* could strike enough spark to kindle a fire!

But toward nightfall of the next day – Larry had lost count of time, nothing existed now but the trudging through wet gulleys and slopes and thorny brushwood – Kennard stopped and turned to him.

"I owe you an apology. This toy of yours is working and I know it now."

"How?" Larry was almost too exhausted to care.

"The air is thinner and the rain is colder. Don't you find it harder to breathe? We must be rising very rapidly now toward the mountain ranges – must have come up several thousand feet in the last few hours alone. Didn't you notice that the western edge of every new gully was higher and harder to climb than the last?"

Larry had thought it was just his own tiredness that had made it seem so; but now that Kennard confirmed it, it seemed indeed that the land had somehow changed character. It was barer; the ridges were longer and steeper, and the abundant berries and nuts and mushrooms had dwindled to a few of the sparser, sourer kind.

"We're getting into the mountains, all right," Kennard said, "and that means we'd better stop early, tonight, and find all the food we can carry. There's nothing in the passes except snow and ice and a few wild birds that nest in the crags and live on the berries up there – berries which happen to be poisonous to humans."

Larry knew he might have found a way out of a couple of serious dilemmas with Terran science, but without Kennard's woodcraft they would both have died many times over.

Food was far from easy to find; they spent hours gathering enough for a sparse supper and a few more meager meals, and during the next day, vegetation diminished almost to nothing. However, Kennard was almost jubilant. If they were actually that near to the mountains, they must be nearing the pass. And that evening, for a little while, like an unexpected gift, the fog and drizzle cleared briefly, and they saw the high peak and the pass that lay below it, shining with the mauve and violet glare of the red sun on the snow, clear before their eyes and less than ten miles away. The brief flash of sun lasted only five minutes or so, but it was long enough for Larry to adjust and check his improvised compass card, take an exact bearing on the pass, and lay out a proper course. After that, whenever any steep slope or rock-ledge forced them to deviate from a chosen direction, he marked it and could correct for it; so that now, instead of going in roughly the right direction, he knew they were going direct for their destination.

But, vindicated though he was in Kennard's eyes, the going was rough now, and getting rougher. There were steep rock-slopes on which they had to scramble on all fours, clutching for handholds on slippery ledges; and once they had to traverse a two-inch-wide track above a cliff-face that left Larry pale and sweating with terror. Kennard took these mock-scrambles quite in stride, and was getting back some of his old, arrogant assurance of leadership, and it bothered Larry. Damn it, it wasn't his fault that he hadn't been trained to climb rock-faces, nor did it make him a passive follower, just because heights of this sort made him sick and dizzy. He gritted his teeth, vowing to himself that anywhere Kennard led, he'd follow – even though it seemed that Kennard could often have chosen easier paths, and was trying to re-establish his own leadership of the expedition by showing off his own superior mountain-craft.

Their provisions ran out that night; they slept, hungry, cold and wet, on a frost-rimed slope a little more level than most – or rather, Kennard slept; Larry had trouble even in breathing. The morning dawned, and long before it was full light, Kennard stirred. He said, "I know you're not asleep. We may as well start. If we're lucky we'll reach the pass before noon." In the bleak morning dimness Larry could not see his friend's face, but he did not need to see. The emotions there were as clear to him as if he were inside Kennard's mind: *On the other side of the passes, there is food, and inhabited country, and warmth, and people to turn to for help. But the pass is going to be hard going. I wouldn't like doing it even with a couple of experienced guides to help. If it doesn't snow, we might get through – if the snow's not already too deep. Can the Terran boy hold out? He's already about exhausted. If he gives in now . . .*

And the despair in that thought suddenly overwhelmed Larry; Kennard was thinking, *If he gives out now, I'll be alone . . . and it will all be for nothing . . .*

Larry wondered suddenly if he were imagining all this, if the height and the hardship were affecting his own mind. This sort of mental eavesdropping didn't make sense. Also,

134

it embarrassed him. He tried, desperately, to close his mind against it, but Kennard's misgivings were leaking through all barriers:

Can Larry hold out? Can he make it? Have I got strength enough for both of us?

Silently, grimly, Larry resolved that if one of them gave out, it would not be himself. He was cold, hungry and wet, but by damn, he'd show this arrogant Darkovan aristocrat something.

Damn it! He was sick of being helped along and treated like the burden and the weaker one!

Terrans weak? Hadn't the Terrans been the first to cross space! Hadn't they taken the blind leap in the dark, before the stardrives, traveling years and years between the stars, ships disappearing and never being heard of again, and yet the race from Terra had spread through all inhabited worlds! Kennard could be proud of his Darkovan heritage and bravery. But there was something to be proud of in the Terrans, too! They had, in a way, their own arrogance, and it was just as reasonable as the Darkovan arrogance.

Here he had assumed, all along, that he was somehow inferior because, on a Darkovan world and in a Darkovan society, he was a burden to Kennard. Suppose it was reversed? Kennard did not understand the workings of a compass. He would be utterly baffled at the drives of a spaceship or a surface-car.

But even if he died here in the mountain passes, he was going to show Kennard that where a Darkovan could lead a Terran could follow! And then, damn it, when they got back to *his* world, he'd challenge Kennard to try following *him* a while in the world of the Terrans – and see if a Darkovan could follow where a Terran led!

He got up, grinned wryly, turned his pockets inside out in the hope of a stray crumb of food – there wasn't one – and said, "The sooner the better."

The grade was steeper now, and there began to be snow underfoot; they went very carefully, guarding against a sideslip that could have meant a ghastly fall. His injured arm felt numbed and twice it slipped on handholds, but he proudly refused Kennard's offers of help.

135

"I'll manage," he said, tight-mouthed.

They came to one dreadful stretch where frost-sheathed stones littered a high ledge without a sign of a track; Kennard, who was leading, set his foot tentatively on the ledge, and it crumbled beneath him, sending pebbles crashing down in a miniature rockslide whitened with powdery snow. He staggered and reeled at the edge of the abyss, but even before he swayed Larry had moved, catching the flash of fear at the touch, and grabbed and held him, hard – the older boy's weight jerking his hurt arm almost from the socket – until Kennard could recover his balance. They clung together, gasping, Kennard with fear and relief and Larry with mingled fright and pain; something had snapped in the injured shoulder and his arm hung stiff and immovable at his side, sending shudders of agony down his side when he as much as moved a finger.

Kennard finally wiped his brow. "Zandru's hells, I thought I was gone," he muttered. "Thanks, Lerrys. I'm all right now. You – " He noted Larry's immobility. "What's the trouble?"

"My arm," Larry managed to get out, shakily.

Kennard touched it with careful fingers, drew a deep whistle. He moved his fingertips over it, his face intent and concentrated. Larry felt a most strange, burning itch deep in his bones under the touch; then Kennard, without a word of warning, suddenly seized the shoulder and gave it a violent, agonizing twist, Larry yelled in pain; he couldn't help it. But as the pain subsided, he realised what Kennard had done.

Kennard nodded. "I had to slip the damned thing back into the socket before it froze the muscles around it. Or it would have taken three men to hold you down while they worked it back into place," he said.

"How did you know – ?"

"Deep-probed," Kennard said briefly. "I can't do it often, or very long. But – " he hesitated, did not finish his sentence. Larry heard it anyhow: *I owed you that much. But damn it, now we're both exhausted!*

"And we've still got that devilish ledge to cross," he said aloud. He began unfastening his belt; tugged briefly at Larry's.

136

Larry, curiously, watched him buckle them together and slip the ends around their wrists.

"Shame you can't use your left hand," he said tersely. "Too bad they found out you were left-handed. Now, we'll start across. Let me lead. This is a hell of a place for your first lesson in climbing this kind of a rock-ledge, but here it is. Always have at least three things all together hanging on. Never move one foot without the other foot and both hands anchored. And the same with either hand." His unfinished sentence again was perfectly clear to Larry: *Both our lives are in his hands, because he's the weakest.*

For the rest of his life, Larry remembered the agonizing hour and a half it took them to cross the twenty-foot stretch of rock-strewn ledge. There were places where the least movement started showers of rocks and snow; yet they could only cling together like limpets to their handholds and to the face of the rock. Above and below was sheer cliff; there was no help there, and if they retraced their steps to find an easier way, they would never get across. Half a dozen times, Larry slipped and the belt jerking them back together saved him from a very long drop into what looked like nothingness and fog below. Halfway across, a thin fine powdery snow began to fall, and Kennard swore in words Larry couldn't even begin to follow.

"That was all we needed!" Suddenly he seemed to brighten up, and placed his next foot more cautiously. "Well, Larry, this is it – this has got to be the worst. Nothing worse than this could possibly happen. From now, things can only get better. Come on – left foot this time. Try that greyish hunk of rock. It looks solid enough."

But at last they were on firm ground again, dropping down as they were in the snow, exhausted, to breathe deep and slow and gasp like runners just finished with a ten-mile race. Kennard, accustomed to the mountains, was as usual the first to recover, and stood up, his voice jubilant.

"I told you it would get better! Look, Larry!"

He pointed. Above them the pallid and snowy light showed them the pass, less than a hundred feet away, leading between rock-sheltered banks – a natural walkway, deeply banked with the falling snow, but sloping only gradually so that they could walk erect.

"And on the other side of that pass, Larry, there are people – my people – friends, who will help us. Warmth and food and fire and – " he broke off. "It seems too good to be true."

"I'd settle for dry feet and something hot to eat," Larry said, then froze, while Kennard still moved toward the pass. The terrible, creeping tension he had felt just before their capture by the trailmen was with him again. It gripped him by the throat; forced him to run after Kennard, grabbing at him with his good arm, holding him back by main force. He couldn't speak; he could hardly breathe with the force of it. The wave surged and crested, the precognition, the foreknowing of terrible danger . . .

It broke. He could breathe again. He gasped and caught at Kennard and pointed and heard the older boy shriek aloud, but the shriek was lost in the siren screaming wail that rose and echoed in the rocky pass. Above them, a huge and ugly craning head, bare of feathers, eyeless and groping, snaked upward, followed by a huge, ungainly body, dimly shining with phosphorescent light. It bore down upon them, clumsily but with alarming speed, cutting off their approach to the pass. The siren-like wailing scream rose and rose until it seemed to fill the air and all the world.

It *had* been too good to be true.

The pass was a nest of one of the evil banshee-birds.

XI

For an instant, in blind panic, Larry whirled, turning to run. The speed with which the banshee caught the change in direction of movement paralyzed him again with terror, but during that split second of immobility, he felt a flash of hope. Kennard had begun to run, stumbling in helpless panic; Larry took one leap after him, wrenching him back, hard.

"*Freeze*," he whispered, urgently. "It senses movement and warmth! Keep perfectly still!"

As Kennard struggled to free himself, he muttered swiftly, "Sorry, pal," swung back his fist and socked Kennard, hard, on the point of the chin. The boy – exhausted, worn, defenseless – collapsed into the snowbank and lay there, motionless, too stunned to rise or to do more than stare, resentfully, at Larry. Larry flung himself down, too, and lay without moving so much as a muscle.

The bird stopped in mid-rush, turning its blind head confusedly from side to side. It blundered back and forth for a moment, its trundling walk and the trailing wings giving it the ungainly look of a huge fat cloaked man. It raised its head and gave forth that terrible, paralyzing wail again.

That's it, Larry thought, resisting the impulse to stuff his hands over his ears. Things hear that awful noise and they run – and the thing *feels them moving!* It's got something like the electrostatic fields of the *kyrri* – only what it senses is their movement, and their smell.

In this snowbank . . .

Very slowly, moving a fraction of an inch at a time, fearing that even the slightest rapid motion might alert the banshee again, he scrabbled slowly in his pocket for his medical kit. It was almost empty, but there might just be enough of the strongly chemical-smelling antiseptic so that they would not smell like anything alive – or, he thought grimly, good to eat.

"Kennard," he whispered, "can you hear me? Don't move a muscle now. But when I slop this stuff around, dive into that snowbank – and burrow as if your life depended on it." *It probably does,* he was thinking.

"*Now!*"

The smell of the chemical was pungent and sharp; the banshee, moving its phosphorescent head against the wind, made strange jolting motions of distaste. It turned and blundered away, and in that moment Larry and Kennard began to dig frantically into the snowbank, throwing up snow behind them, scrabbling it back over their bodies.

They were safe – for the moment. But how would they get across the pass?

Then he remembered Kennard's earlier words about the banshees. They're night-birds, torpid in the sunlight. The phosphorescence of their heads proved that they were no creatures of normal sunlight.

If they could live through the night . . .

If they didn't freeze to death . . .

If some other banshee couldn't feel their warmth through the snow around them . . .

If the sun shone tomorrow, brightly enough to quiet the great birds . . .

If all these things happened, then they just *might* live through their last hurdle.

If not . . .

Suddenly all these *ifs*, coming at him like blasts of fear from Kennard, stirred fury in him. Damn it, there *had* to be a way through! And Kennard seemed to have given up; he was just lying there in the snow, silent, apparently ready for death.

But they hadn't come so far together to die here, at the last. Damn it, he'd get them over that pass if he had to burrow through the damned snowbank with his bare hands . . .

The banshee seemed to have gone; cautiously, he lifted his head, ever so slightly, from the snowbank. Then, thinking better of it, he plastered the freezing stuff over his head before lifting it up, quickly surveying the pass above them.

140

Less than a hundred feet. If they could somehow crawl through the snow . . .

Urgently, he shook Kennard's shoulder. The Darkovan boy did not move. The last terror had evidently finished his endurance. He muttered, "Right back where we were – when we left Cyrillon's castle – "

Larry's fury exploded. "So after dragging me halfway across the country, within the sight of safety you're going to lie here and die?"

"The banshees – "

"Oh, your own god Zandru take the banshees! We'll get through them or else we won't, but by damn we'll *try!* You Darkovans – so proud of your courage when it's a matter of individual bravery! As long as you could be a *hero*" – he flayed Kennard, deliberately, intently, with his words – "you were brave as could be! When you could make me look small! But now when you have to work *with* me, you konk out and lie down to die! And Valdir thinks he can do anything with your people? What the hell – his own son can't shut up and listen and co-operate! He's got to be a goddam hero, or he won't play, and just lies down to die!"

Kennard swallowed. His eyes blazed fire, and Larry braced himself for another outburst of that flaying, dreadful Alton rage, but it was checked before it began. Kennard clenched his fists, but he spoke grimly, through his teeth.

"I'll kill you for that, some day – but right now, you'll see whether a Terran can lead an Alton on his own world. Try it."

"That's the way to talk," Larry said, deliberately jovial to infuriate Kennard's despairing dignity. "If we're going to die anyhow, we might as well do it while we're *doing* something about it! To hell with dying with dignity! Make the blasted beast fight for his dinner if he wants it – kicking and scratching!"

Kennard laid his hand on his knife. He said, "He'll get a fight – "

Larry gripped his wrist, "*No!* Warmth and movement are what he senses! Damn you and your heroics! Common sense is what we need. Hell, I know you're *brave*, but try showing some brains too!"

Kennard froze. He said through barely moving lips, "All right. I said I'd follow your lead. What do I do now?"

Larry thought fast. He had pulled Kennard out of his fit of despair, but now he had to *offer* something. If he was going to take the lead, he had to lead – and do it damned fast!

The banshee sensed warmth and movement.

Therefore, it must be something like the *kyrri*; and the only way to outwit it was with cold, and stillness. But they could freeze to death and it could outwait them. Or else –

The idea struck him.

"Listen! You run one way and I'll run the other – "

Kennard said, "Drawing lots for death? I accept that. Whichever one of us he takes, the other goes free?"

"*No*, idiot!" Larry hadn't even thought of that. It was a noble Darkovan concept and honorable, but it seemed damned unnecessary. "We both get free or neither. No, what I'm thinking about is to *confuse* the damned thing. I move. He's drawn off after me. Then I stop, burrow in a snowbank, stay still as a mouse – and while he's trying to scent me again, *you* start running around. Somewhere else. He'll start to move in *that* direction. Then you freeze and I start again. Maybe we can confuse him, keep him running back and forth long enough to get across the pass."

Kennard looked at him with growing excitement. "It just might *work*."

"All right, get ready – *freeze!*"

Larry jumped up and started running. He saw the huge lumbering bird twitch toward him as by a tropism, then come speeding. He yelled to Kennard, diving into a snowbank, scrabbled frantically in and lay still, not daring to move or hardly to breathe.

He felt, rather than seeing, the great bird stop short, clumsily twitch around, jerking in irritation. How had its prey gotten over *there?* Kennard dashed about twenty yards toward the pass, shouted and dived. Larry jumped up again. This time he tried to run too far; the evil creature's foul breath was actually hot on his neck and his flesh crawled with anticipation of the swift, disemboweling clawing stroke. He fell into the snow, burrowed in and lay still. The siren wail of the confused bird rose, filling the air with screaming

142

terror, and Larry thought, *Oh, God, don't let Kennard panic again* . . .

He raised his head cautiously, watched Kennard dive down, rose again and dashed. The bird twitched, began to lumber back, suddenly howled and began to dash madly in circles, its huge head flopping and flapping.

The banshee howl fell to terrified little yelps and the creature fell on its back, twitching.

Larry yelled to Kennard, "Come on! Run!" He was remembering psychology courses. Animals, especially very stupid animals, faced with a situation wholly frustrating and outside their experience, go completely to pieces and crack up. The banshee was lying in the snow squealing with a complete nervous breakdown.

They ran, gasping and trembling. The clouds seemed suddenly to thin and lift, and the pale Darkovan sun burst suddenly forth in morning brilliance.

Larry hauled himself up, exhausted, to the summit of the pass. He rested there, gasping, Kennard at his side.

Before them lay a trail downward, and far away, a countryside patched with quiet fields, smoke rising from small houses and hearthstones, the tree-laden slopes of low foothills and green leaves.

Exhausted, wearied, famished, they stood there feasting their eyes on the beauty and richness of the country that lay below. Kennard pointed. Far away, almost out of sight range, a gray spire just visible through the mist rose upward.

"Castle Hastur – and we've won!"

"Not yet," Larry said, warningly. "It's a long way off yet. And we'd better get right out of the high snows while the sun is bright enough to keep any of that big fellow's sisters and his cousins and his aunts from coming around!"

"You're right," Kennard said, sobering instantly, and they trudged off down the narrow trail, not really liking to think what had made it. But at least the sun was bright, and for the moment they were safe.

Larry had leisure to feel, now, how weary he was. His dislocated shoulder ached like the very devil. His feet were cold and hot by turns – he was sure he had frostbite – and his fingers were white and cold from scrabbling in the snow. He sucked them and slapped them together, trying hard to keep from moaning with the pain of returning circulation. But he kept pace with Kennard. He'd taken over the leadership – and he wasn't going to give out now!

The slopes on this side were heavily wooded, but the woods were mostly conifers and spruce, and there was still no sign of food. Lower down on the slope, they found a single tree laden with apples, damp and wrinkled after the recent storm, but still edible; they filled their pockets, and sat down to eat side by side. Larry thought of the peaceful time, so few days ago really, when they had sat side by side like this, before the alarm of forest-fire. What years he seemed to have lived, and what hills and valleys he had crossed – figuratively as well as literally – since then!

Kennard was frowning at him and Larry remembered, with an absolute wrench of effort, that they had exchanged harsh words in the pass.

Kennard said, "Now that we are out of danger – you spoke words to me beyond forgiveness. We are *bredin,* but I'm going to beat them down your throat!"

Oh no! Not that again!

"Forget it," he said. "I was trying to save both our lives; I didn't have time to be tactful."

Kennard is sulking because I saved our lives when he couldn't. He wants to settle it the Darkovan way – with a fight. Larry said, aloud, "I won't fight with you, Ken. You saved my life too many times. I would no more hit you than – than my own father."

Kennard looked at him, trembling with rage. "Coward!"

Larry took a deliberate bite out his apple. It was sour. He said, "Calling me names won't hurt me. Go ahead, if it makes you feel better." Then he added, gently, "Anyhow, what would it prove, except that you are stronger than I? I've never doubted that, even for a moment. We'd *still* be in this thing together. And after coming through all this together – why should we end it with a fight, as if we were enemies instead of friends?" Deliberately, he used the word *bredin* again. He held out his hand. "If I said anything to hurt you, I'm sorry. You've hurt me a time or two, so even by your own codes we're even. Let's shake hands and forget it."

Kennard hesitated, and for a flooding, bitter moment Larry feared he would rebuff the gesture, and for that same moment Larry almost wished they had died together in the pass. They had grown as close as if their minds were one – and being closed away, now, hurt like a knife.

Then, like sunlight breaking through a cloud, Kennard smiled. He held out both hands and clasped Larry's in them.

"Have another apple," was all he said. But it was enough.

XII

The trail downward was hard, rough going; but with the fear of the banshees behind them, and Larry's growing skill at rock-climbing, they managed the descent better than the ascent. Weary, half starved, Larry felt a relief all out of measure to their present situation – for in a trackless, almost foodless forest, they had still several days walking to cover before they came to inhabited country. They had seen it from the pass, but it was far away.

And yet the optimism seeded in him, growing higher and higher, like a cresting wave, like . . .

Like the growth of his fear when they had been in the acute danger of capture by the trailmen and he had not yet known it!

What kind of freak am I? How did I get it? I'm no telepath. And it can't be learned.

Yet, he felt this cresting, flooding hope – almost like a great joy. The woods seemed somehow greener, the sky a more brilliant mauve, the red sun to shine with brilliance and glory overhead. Could it be only relief at escape? Or –

"Kennard, do you suppose we might meet a hunting party who are in these woods?"

Kennard, learned in woodcraft, chuckled wryly. "Who would hunt here – and what for? There seems to be not a sign of game in these woods, though later we may find fruit or berries. You look damned optimistic," he added, rather sullenly still.

He's mad because I faced him down. But he'll get over it.

They scrambled their way to the lip of a rocky rise in the land, and stood looking down into a green valley, so beautiful that in the grip of this unexplained joy Larry stood almost ecstatically, entranced by the trees, by the little stream that ran silver at the botoom. Songbirds were singing. And

146

through the birdsong, and the clear-running water, there was another sound – a clear voice, singing. The voice of a human creature.

In another moment, through the trees, a tall figure appeared. He was singing, in a musical, unknown tongue.

Kennard stood half-enraptured. He whispered, "A *chieri!*" Human?

The creature was, indeed, human in form, though tall and of such a fragile slenderness that he seemed even more so. He? Was the creature a woman? The voice had been clear and high, like a woman's voice. It wore a long robe of some gleaming grayish silky substance. Long pale hair lay across the slim shoulders. The beckoning hand was white and almost translucent in the sunlight, and the bones of the face had an elfin, delicate, triangular beauty.

Flying around the head of the elfin creature were a multitude of singing birds, whose melodious voices mingled with that of the *chieri*. Suddenly the *chieri* looked sharply upward, and called in a clear voice. "You there, you evil tramplers! Go, before you frighten my birds, or I put an ill word on you!"

Kennard stepped forward, raising his hands in a gesture of surrender and respect. Larry remembered the respect the Darkovan boy had shown Lorill Hastur. This was more than respect it was deference, it was almost abasement.

"Child of grace," he said, half-audibly, "we mean no harm to you or your birds. We are lost and desperate. My friend is hurt. If you can give us no help, give us at least none of your evil will."

The beautiful, epicene face, suddenly clear in the patch of sunlight, softened. Raising the thin hands, the *chieri* let the birds fly free, in a whirling cloud. Then the creature beckoned to them, but as they began to trudge wearily down the slope, it ran lightly upward to them.

"You are hurt! You have cuts and bruises; you are hungry, you have come through that dreadful pass haunted by evil things – ?"

"We have," Kennard said faintly, "and we have crossed all the country from the castle of Cyrillon des Trailles."

"What are you?"

"I am Comyn," Kennard said, with his last scraps of dignity,

147

"of the Seven Domains. This – this lad is my friend and *bredu*. Give us a shelter, or at least no harm!"

The *chieri*'s fair and mobile face was gentle. "Forgive me. Evil things come sometimes from the high passes, and foul my clear pools and frighten my birds. They fear me, fortunately – but I do not always see them. But you – " The *cheri* looked at them, a clear piercing gray gaze, and said, "You mean no harm to us."

The glance held Larry's eyes spellbound. Kennard whispered, "Are you a mighty *leronis?*"

"I am of the *chieri*. Are you wiser, son of Alton?"

You know my name?"

"I know your name, Kennard son of Valdir, and your friend's. Yet I have none of your Comyn powers. But you are weary and your friend in pain; so no more talk now. Can you walk a steep path?" The *chieri* seemed almost apologetic. "I must guard myself, in this land."

Larry, drawing himself upright, said, "I can go where I must."

Kennard said, "You lend us grace, child of light. And blessed was the lord of Carthon when he met with Kierestelli beside the wells of Reuel."

"Is that tale still known?" The alien, elfin face was merry. "But time enough later for tales and old legends, son of the Seven Domansa. No more talk now. Come."

The *chieri* turned, taking an upward path. It was a long climb and Larry was sweating in exhaustion, his injured arm feeling ready to drop off, before they reached the top. At the end, Kennard was half carrying him. But even Kennard was too weary to do more, and the *chieri* came, an arm around each, and supported them. Frail, almost boneless as the creature looked, it was incredibly strong.

They came out upon a flat space, screened with living boughs, and entered a door of woven wicker into the strangest room he had ever seen.

The floor was of earth, not mud or of sun-dried brick, but carpeted thickly with grass and living moss in which a cricket chirped; it felt warm and fragrant under their feet.

The *chieri* bent and removed his sandals, and at his signal, the boys removed their wet and soaking boots and worn socks. The grass felt comfortable to their weary feet.

The walls were of woven wicker, screened lightly with thin hangings of cloth, heavy but not coarse, which admitted light but could not be seen through. In the roof of thatch, vines with great trumpet-shaped blossoms were growing, which pervaded the whole place with a fragrance of green and growing things. It smelled fresh, and sweet. An opened door at the back led to an enclosed garden where a fountain splashed into a stone bowl, running out and away in a little rivulet. A fire burned there in a small brazier of hardened clay, and over it was a metal crane on which a steaming kettle swung, giving forth a good smell of hot food. The lads felt their eyes watering at this steam. Furniture there was little, save for a bench or chest or two, and at the edge of the room an upright loom with a strung web on it.

As they entered, the *chieri* raised its hands, saying in its clear voice, "Enter in a good hour, and let no fear or danger trouble you within these walls." That done, it turned to Larry saying, "You are hurt and in pain, and you flee from evil things. I sensed your minds within the pass. I will ask no more till you have had rest and food."

It went to the brazier, and Kennard, sinking down on the grass wearily, said, "Who are you, child of grace?"

"You may call me Narad-zinie," said the *chieri*, "which is my name among your people. My own would be strange to your ears and overlong." From a chest it took silver cups, plainly but beautifully worked, and poured drink into them. It offered a cup to each. Larry tasted; it was delicious, but very strong wine. He hesitated a moment, then his weariness and his thirst overcame him; he drank it up anyhow. Almost at once the sense of complete exhaustion left him and he watched alertly as the *chieri* moved the kettle aside from the brazier.

"Porridge is slim food alone for footsore travelers," it said. "I will make you some cakes as well. No more wine until you have eaten, though! Meanwhile – " It gestured at the fountain, and Larry, suddenly abashed at his dirty and torn clothes, went to wash and douse his head under the fountain. Kennard followed suit.

When Larry came back, something like pancakes were

149

baking on a flat griddle over the brazier. They smelled so good that his mouth watered. The *chieri* brought them food on flat, beautifully carved wooden trays, and there were also bowls of porridge, the flat pancakes which had a yeasty, puffy texture, bowls of hot milk, honey and what tasted like cheese. The flavors were oddly pungent, but the boys were far too hungry to care; they demolished everything in sight, and the *chieri* brought them second helpings of pancakes and honey. Replete at last, they leaned back and surveyed the room, and Larry's first words were oddly irrelevant.

"The trailmen might evolve something like this, instead of what you fear, Kennard."

The *chieri* answered for Kennard. "The trail-folk, in the far-back times, were our kinfolk, but then we left the trees and built fire, they feared it and our ways moved apart. They are our younger brothers, to grow more slowly in wisdom. But perhaps it is time, indeed, for what this child of two worlds has done."

Larry stared up at the alien's strange beautiful face. "You – know all this?"

"The Comyn powers are *chieri* powers, little brother," the *chieri* said. It stretched out its long body on the green turf. "I suppose you have no patience with long tales, so I will say only this, Kennard – the *chieri* lived on Darkover long before you Terrans came, to drive us into the deep and deeper woods."

Kennard said, "But I am not Terran," and Larry felt his amazed anger. "Larry is the Terran!"

The *chieri* smiled. "I forgot," he said gently, "that to your people, the passing of a lifetime is as a sleep and a sleep to our folk. Children of Terra are you both. I was here, a youngling of my people, when the first ship from Terra arrived, a lost ship and broken, and your people were forced to remain here. The time came when they forgot their origins; but the name they gave to this world – Darkover – indeed reflects their speech and their customs."

It was a strange tale he told, and Kennard and Larry, lying at ease and almost in disbelief, listened while the *chieri* told his tale.

The Terran ship had been one of the first early starships

to cross space. Their crew, some hundred men and women, had been forced to remain, and after dozens of generations – which had seemed like only a little while to the *chieri* folk – they had spread over most of the planet.

"There is a tale you spoke of," the *chieri* said, "of the lord of Carthon – one of your people. Kennard – who met with a woman of my folk Kierestelli; and she loved him, and bore him a son, and therewith she died, but the blood had mixed. And this son, Hastur, loved a maiden of your people, Cassilda, and from this admixture in their seven sons came the Seven Domains in which you take such pride."

Interbreeding to produce these new telepathic powers in greater intensity had led to seven pure strains of telepathy, each with its own Domain, or family; and each with its own kind of *laran*, or psi power.

"The Hasturs. The Aillards. The Ridenow. The Elhalyn. The Altons – your clan, young Kennard. And the Aldaran."

"The Aldaran," said Kennard with a trace of bitterness, "were exiled from the Comyn – and they sold our world to the Terrans!"

The *chieri*'s beautiful face was strange. "You mean, when the Terrans came again, for the second time, the Aldaran first welcomed their long-forgotten brothers to their own people who had forgotten their ancestry," he said. "Perhaps among the Aldarans, their Terran heritage was never forgotten. But as for you, little son of Darkover and of Terra" – and he looked at Larry with great gentleness – "you are weary; you should sleep. Yet I know very well why you are in haste. Even now – " his face became distant – "Valdir Alton answers for your fate to these new Terrans who have also forgotten that these men of Darkover are their brothers. As, indeed, all folk are brothers, though there are many, many times when they forget it. And because you are both of my people, I will help you – though I would love to speak more to you. For I am old, and of a dying race. Our women bear no more children, and one day the *chieri* will be only a memory, living on only in the blood of those, their conquerers." He sighed. "Beautiful were our forests in those days. Yet time and change come to all men and all worlds, and you are right to speak with reverence of Kierestelli and to call Cassilda blessed, who

151

first mingled blood with blood and thus assured that the *chieri* would survive in blood if never in memory. But I am old – I talk too much. I should act instead."

He got to his feet. With those strange gray eyes – eyes like the eyes of Lorill Hastur, Larry realized – he enspelled them both, until nothing but those gray eyes remained; space whirled away and reeled –

Bright hot light struck their eyes. Yellow light. They were standing on a brilliantly tiled floor in a brightly glassed-in room overlooking the spaceport of Darkover, and before them, in attitudes of defiance, stood Valdir Alton, Commander Reade – and Larry's father.

XIII

They had slept. They were rested and fed and re-clothed, Kennard this time in some spare garments of Larry's and once again they sat before Valdir Alton and Wade Montray and Commander Reade, finishing the tale of their adventures.

Valdir said at last, his face very grave, "I have heard of the *chieri*-folk; but I did not know that any of them still lived, even in the deep woods. And what you tell me of our mixed heritage is strange – and troubling," he added honestly, his eyes meeting those of Wade Montray with a confused newness in them. "Yet the old *chieri* spoke only a truth I already knew. Time and change come to all worlds, even to ours. And if our sons could cross the mountains together in harmony – and neither alone could have lived, but both needed the other's ways – then perhaps our worlds are the same."

"Father," said Kennard gravely, "I decided something on the way back. Don't be angry; it's something I must do. I will do it with your consent now, or without your consent when I come of age. But I am going to take ship for Terra, and learn all that they can teach me there, in their schools. And after me, there will be others."

Valdir Alton looked troubled; but finally he nodded.

"You are a man, free to choose," he said, "and perhaps the choice is wise. Time only will tell. And you, Lerrys," he added, for Larry had raised his head to speak.

"I want to learn your languages and your history, sir. It's foolish, to live here without learning them – not only for me, but for all the Terrans who come here."

Valdir nodded again, gravely. "Then you shall do it as a son in my house," he said. "You and my son are *bredin*; our house is yours."

"Ah, some day," Reade said, "a school will be established for sons of both worlds to learn about the other." He looked wryly at the boys and said, "I appoint you both Special Consultants on the Bureau of Terran-Darkovan Liaison. Hurry up and finish that interplanetary education of yours, boys."

"One more thing," Valdir said. "I think we need to learn from Terra about such things as forest fires, and what to do about bandits and banshees. And then, to use the knowledge in our own way." He looked straight at Wade Montray and said, "Forgive me for intruding, but I am Alton. I think you should tell your son, now, why the *chieri* could call them both his kindred."

Wade Montray stood before his son. "You've grown," he said. "You're a man." Then he wet his lips.

"Larry, you were born on Darkover," he said, "of a woman of the high Darkovan caste of the Aldaran, who forsook her people for me, and returned with me to Terra. For years I would not bring you back. I didn't want you torn apart between two worlds, as I had been. I tried to keep you away from Darkover, but the call was too strong for you. As the call had been too strong for me." His face worked. "So you'll be torn between two alien worlds – as I was – "

"But," Larry said quietly, and he stretched a hand to his father. "Darkovans are not alien. Once they were Earthmen. And Earthmen are akin to Darkovans, even those who have not the *chieri* blood in their veins. The call is not of alien worlds – but of blood brothers, who want to understand one another again. It won't be easy. But" – his eyes sought out Kennard's – "it's a beginning."

Wade Montray nodded, slowly and painfully, and Valdir Alton, suddenly, did a thing unprecedented for a Darkovan aristocrat. Awkwardly, the gesture unpracticed, he held out his hand to Wade Montray, and the two men shook hands, while Commander Reade beamed.

They had, indeed, made a beginning. Trouble would come – as all change brings trouble in its wake. But it was a beginning, and, as with the bringing of fire to the trailmen, the benefits would outweigh the risks.

The first step had been taken.

Larry and Kennard would take the next.

And after them, thousands.

The brother worlds were once again reconciled.

154